THE COMPLETE HISTORY OF WHY I HATE HER

THE COMPLETE HISTORY OF WHY I HATE HER

Jennifer Richard Jacobson

TEEN

A RICHARD JACKSON BOOK
Atheneum Books for Young Readers • *New York London Toronto Sydney*

ATHENEUM BOOKS FOR YOUNG READERS
An imprint of Simon & Schuster Children's Publishing Division
1230 Avenue of the Americas, New York, New York 10020
This book is a work of fiction. Any references to historical events, real people,
or real locales are used fictitiously. Other names, characters, places, and
incidents are products of the author's imagination, and any resemblance to
actual events or locales or persons, living or dead, is entirely coincidental.
Copyright © 2010 by Jennifer Richard Jacobson
ATHENEUM BOOKS FOR YOUNG READERS is a registered trademark of
Simon & Schuster, Inc.
For information about special discounts for bulk purchases, please contact
Simon & Schuster Special Sales at 1-866-506-1949 or
business@simonandschuster.com.
The Simon & Schuster Speakers Bureau can bring authors to your live event.
For more information or to book an event, contact the Simon & Schuster
Speakers Bureau at 1-866-248-3049 or visit our website at
www.simonspeakers.com.
Book design by Lauren Rille
The text for this book is set in Perpetua.
Manufactured in the United States of America
First Edition
10 9 8 7 6 5 4 3 2 1
Library of Congress Cataloging-in-Publication Data
Jacobson, Jennifer, 1958–
The complete history of why I hate her / Jennifer Richard Jacobson.—1st ed.
p. cm.
Summary: Wanting a break from being known only for her sister's cancer,
seventeen-year-old Nola leaves Boston for a waitressing job at a summer
resort in Maine, but soon feels as if her new best friend is taking over her life.
ISBN 978-0-689-87800-8 (hardcover)
[1. Interpersonal relations—Fiction. 2. Identity—Fiction. 3. Resorts—
Fiction. 4. Personality disorders—Fiction. 5. Cancer—Fiction. 6. Sisters—
Fiction. 7. Maine—Fiction.] I. Title.
PZ7.J1529Com 2010
[Fic]—dc22
2008042959
ISBN 978-1-4169-9925-6 (eBook)

FOR DICK JACKSON,
with immense gratitude

Acknowledgments

A thousand thanks to those who read this story multiple times: Mary Atkinson, Jacqueline Davies, Barry Goldblatt (who also happens to be an extraordinary agent), Holly Jacobson, Jane Kurtz, and Dana Walrath. Your dazzling insights and unwavering support led me to the story I needed to tell. (All failures in literary judgment are mine.) Additional thanks go to Toni Buzzeo, Franny Billingsley, Jacqueline Briggs Martin, Dian Curtis Regan, Deborah Wiles, Joanne Stanbridge, and Nancy Werlin for fortuitous discussions and brainstorms. Kudos go to Team Atheneum including Emma Dryden, Carol Chou, Cindy Nixon, Debra Sfetsios, Lauren Rille, and Kiley Frank. And finally, enormous thanks to my editor, Dick Jackson, for both his editorial brilliance and his faith in me.

chapter 1

Song is hanging on my arm, afraid I'm going to slip onto the bus and out of her life as quickly as I made the decision to go. I step back, allowing other passengers to board, trying to keep our good-bye upbeat, trying not to feel like the lousiest sister on the planet.

Those in line near us stare. We're used to it. Song's bald head and skinny body always produce curiosity and contorted, sympathetic expressions. We're like a sappy Lifetime movie wherever we go.

Usually, I see faces of allies. Today I feel as if those faces are judging me.

"Please don't hate me," I say to Song.

"Of course she doesn't hate you," my mother says, stepping closer.

I keep my eyes locked on my little sister. It's hard for our family to remember she's thirteen. She's been through more than most, and although she tries to portray a kick-ass attitude with her holey jeans and punk T-shirts, she still looks like a scrawny little kid.

She won't look me in the eye. Instead, she launches into haiku—a language we've used since she learned the form in third grade:

> *"Off to a reserve*
> *Anyone for lawn bowling?*
> *I'll stay here and puke"*

She means "resort," but I don't correct her. My reply:

> *"Hey, I'll be working.*
> *'Can I get you anything else?'*
> *Just a lowly wench"*

We've had lots of practice turning onlookers into an audience. Makes it easier to deal. Especially today. Especially when saying good-bye seems impossible.

Song continues:

> *"Caviar and cake—"*

She stops herself, unable or unwilling to go on. And then she moves closer. "Don't forget your promise," she whispers.

"Of course not," I say.

She wraps her arms around me—more stronghold than hug.

I hold her for as long as I can take. Then I wiggle out, quickly kiss my mom, and climb onto the bus—picking up the free headphones, though my own are hanging around my neck. *Don't think, don't think, don't think,* I repeat, sliding into a window seat.

A large woman follows, choosing the seat next to mine. I've barely plopped down before she starts packing garbage bags all around me. They're stuffed with clothes, I hope.

"Visiting my brother in Brewer," she says. "No one would see him if I didn't get on a bus once a year. You know?"

I nod and tell her I'm going to Rocky Cove, Maine.

"Rocky Cove?"

"Near Bucks Harbor," I say.

"There's nothing near Bucks Harbor, honey."

Should I tell her about my job? Nah, I don't have the energy. I look out the window to locate Mom and Song but catch a glimpse of my still-surprising reflection instead. I cut my hair off yesterday. Not like Song—I didn't shave my head the way the seventh-grade boys did when they heard doctors had found another tumor. No, I waited until yesterday and then had my long hair cut into a short, crazy bob. I even said yes to red streaks.

"You don't even look like *you*," my mother cried.

3

Mission accomplished. Of course, if I'd had any sense, I would have waited until I got to Maine.

I lean back and glance at a girl about my age, with the long hair I used to have, across the aisle. She catches my eye and smiles.

I smile back.

The woman next to me pulls an open pack of Life Savers from her purse, flicks tobacco off the top one, and offers it to me.

"I'm good," I say.

The girl giggles.

We share a roll of the eyes, and then I turn to the window. We're pulling out of South Station. *Good-bye, Boston.* Mom is waving one arm, throwing kisses with the other.

Song bends her arm at the elbow and raises her hand as if she were taking an oath—or saying, *Stop.* My breath catches.

I want to yell, *No, wait!* and run off the bus and into the arms of my little sister, back into the family cocoon where everyone is waiting, dreading, watching with one eye open at all times. Ready to push back fear—to push back fear and doubt and . . .

But I can't. I need to say, *Yes.* Not yes to another round of Scrabble or yes to *Halloween III* again or yes to "I'll stay home tonight and make sure Song's temp doesn't spike," but yes to—to what? A break.

That's all. Just a break. Two and a half months to see what it would feel like to be, well, *me*.

Here's what saying yes feels like. Like I'm a total coward and courageous at the same time.

"I know he has to work," the woman continues. "I don't expect him to lose hours to pick me up."

I place my hand on the glass and whisper as I've done a thousand times before, *Be strong, Song*.

Please.

Be fierce.

chapter 2

"Do you have a brother?" the woman asks.

I shake my head. Song is definitely not a boy, even if she looks like one. But my seatmate's question simply leads her back to all things her. On and on she talks about the brother she *has* to visit, and she's, seriously, so loud and relentless, people around us groan.

She is not the type of woman, though, to take a hint.

Suddenly, the girl across the aisle jumps up. "Wow!" she says to me. "I can't believe *you* of all people are on this bus! I haven't seen you in . . . how many years has it been?"

Huh?

"You two know each other?" the woman asks.

"We were in the same foster home," says the girl. "We're practically sisters."

"I—I can't believe you're on this bus," I say, hoping that this is a rescue mission and not a case of mistaken identity.

"Do you mind if we trade seats?" the girl asks. "We have so much catching up to do."

The woman sighs but gathers her bags and moves to the other side of the aisle.

Once my savior is settled, she leans over—her long hair creating a tent to block the woman's view—and whispers, "Carly. Carly Whitehouse."

"Nola Werth," I whisper back.

"Next time sit on the aisle. People won't crawl over you, and they won't ask you to move if they can help it." She pulls a water bottle from her bag, which is made from a patchwork of colorful, silky fabrics, and downs a few gulps.

"Sounds like you take the bus a lot," I say, suddenly feeling self-conscious. Carly is one of those girls who exude confidence. Her deer eyes are huge, making her striking in an exotic sort of way. Her clothes are what my cousin Georgia calls "funky chic," which requires an advanced degree in clothing chemistry—knowing what can be combined and what can't. *This is who I want to be*, I think.

"I do take the bus a lot," she says. "My parents are divorced, and I spend half my life traveling between them. How 'bout you?"

"Still together," I say.

"No, I mean do you take the bus often?"

I laugh. "Oh, not really." In other words, never. Except for a couple of family vacations, I've rarely left Massachusetts.

The movie comes on, and I wonder if it would be the polite thing or rude to put on my headphones.

"Ack. I've seen this one," Carly says. "It's so lame."

Headphones off. The last thing I want to be today is lame.

"Is it just me, or is every actress starting to look the same?" I say, tucking one of my legs under me. "I mean, it seems they're all trying to be Blake Lively." I'm hoping to sound as if this just occurred to me. In truth, Song and I talk about it practically every time we click on a trailer.

"Depends on the movie," says Carly, turning toward me. "If an actor is playing in a comedy—even a romantic comedy—she'll go blond. When she plays an edgier, 'I want the Oscar' role, she'll go dark."

"Really?" I'm pleased to have come up with a topic that seems halfway entertaining. "So, with my hair, I wouldn't get the guy, but I could be the intense, neurotic—"

"Suicidal woman," she finishes for me.

Well, yes, I think. "Virginia Woolf." (Okay, so I haven't read any of her work, but I did see the movie about her.)

"You got it," says Carly.

"What about you? Your hair is almost blond."

"Dirty blond. I'm the doomed victim gone in the first shot. The dispensable one."

"No way," I say, trying to keep the envy out of my voice. "You get all the guys."

"Girls, could you lower your voices?" my former seatmate complains. "Some of us are trying to watch." She points to the screen ahead.

We can't help it. Her snarl only makes us laugh louder.

Carly and I talk most of the two hours from Boston to Portland, covering all of the obvious ground: classes (both of us barely made it through our APs this year); fall sports (Carly: field hockey, me: running); boys (Carly: many passionate affairs, me: none worth mentioning); virginity (Carly: see above, me: intend to lose mine this summer . . . just kidding . . . well, maybe not).

In Portland the bus stops so we can get off and stretch. Carly makes a call. I use the restroom and then think of calling home, but instead head outside into the cool evening air. Beyond the parking lot I see the lights of the city, and for a brief moment I think, *I could walk away and not a soul in this world would know where I am.* Both surprising and exhilarating.

"There you are," says Carly, startling me. We board the bus and continue on to Bangor.

My summer has begun.

chapter 3

I spot the owner of the Rocky Cove Inn from his website photos—a tall, thin man, with rounded shoulders and wire-rimmed glasses. "Mr. Lovell?"

"You must be Nola," he says, shaking my hand. "You look different from your application picture."

I touch my red-streaked, cropped hair, hoping he isn't sorry he hired me.

"Isn't she wonderful?" Carly says, appearing from behind us. She slings an arm around my shoulder.

"This is Carly," I tell him. "We came from Boston together."

"Call me Pete." He holds out his hand to Carly. "Everyone does. And this urchin is Stella," he says, introducing a towheaded kid adhered to the back of his leg.

"Hi, Miss Stella!" says Carly.

"Do you have a job Downeast too, Carly?" Pete asks.

I wait for her to tell him she lives here but—

"Well, I did," she says. "But it fell through at the last minute. I was going to be a nanny. But the woman who hired me called to say she wasn't spending the summer in Maine after all. Shouldn't take me too long to find another job, though. At least, I hope people are still looking for summer help."

"True enough," says Pete. "Can I drop you somewhere?"

"No thanks," Carly says. "I'll grab a bite and then make my way home."

"I'm taking Nola across the street to Papa's if you'd like to join us. It's still preseason at the inn—chef's night off."

"Pizza, pizza, pizza!" yells Stella.

"Who can pass up Papa's?" says Carly.

I'm so glad Carly is coming along. I didn't know I'd be having dinner with my boss, and I'd be so nervous—trying to make a good impression alone. This way a little of Carly might rub off on me.

Pete tells me the history of Rocky Cove (how before it was a resort, it was a granite quarry and a supplier of ice; blocks of ice were cut from the lake, stored in what's now one of the cabins, and then shipped off to China by sea) while Carly helps Stella pick the "ronis" off the pizza, pour a third glass of water from the plastic pitcher, and sing all of the verses of "On Top of Spaghetti."

"I can see you'd be a good nanny," says Pete.

"Just one of my many talents," she says. "I've also waitressed, painted houses, worked as a lifeguard."

"Too bad we don't have any openings, but give me your number in case."

"Great," says Carly, grabbing a napkin and one of the crayons the waitress left for Stella. "This is my cell."

As we make our way to the door, Carly runs into an old friend. We say quick good-byes, and I wonder if I'll see her again.

Pete chatters all the way to Rocky Cove, and when he pauses, Stella fills in. But the drive seems long—longer, darker, and windier than I expected—or maybe I'm just anxious to finally get there. I know the place is upscale—only resorts provide room and board for waitresses. And this one has two beaches, ocean and lakeside. It sounds incredible. But that isn't the reason I chose it over the others. No, only Rocky Cove accepts waitresses without prior experience. *We like to train our help,* Pete wrote.

A bumpy dirt driveway . . . and there it is. The inn in the full moonlight looks big and boxy, like an old-fashioned school but with an open porch on all sides (to catch summer breezes at every window, Pete tells me). Only the porch and one of the rooms on the third floor is lit, but the place has that promise of summer easiness. *Welcome to your dream life,* the inn seems to be saying. *Sit here where you belong.* It is the kind of place that makes you feel lucky even though you've done nothing more than walk up the steps.

"Tomorrow I'll give you the grand tour," Pete says, "but for now I'll just show you the barn."

The barn?

"Me too, Daddy?" Stella asks.

Pete takes her hand.

We backtrack along the driveway to a structure hidden in the trees. Pete leads me across another broad wooden porch, through glass doors, and into a room that *is* barnlike. There's a large stone fireplace at one end, and wicker benches and chairs around tables in the center. The walls are lined with plywood shelves holding board games and playing cards. An ancient computer sits in one corner.

"This is where guests come on rainy days," Pete says, continuing out a back door into a large maintenance room. Lawn mowers, gasoline, paint cans, tools of all shapes and sizes crowd the floor.

"Hello?" yells Pete at the base of a narrow staircase. "Anyone home?"

No answer.

"Looks like everyone's out for the evening," he says as we climb to a cluster of bedrooms and a tiny bathroom built under the eaves.

Stella grabs my hand and shows me around. I may be in a barn, but the rooms are instantly recognizable. They look like mine looks most of the time. Hair dryers, clothes, makeup, and discarded shoes everywhere. But where are the girls? We passed through a town Pete identified as Blue Hill, though it sure didn't look as if anything was going on there.

I feel a pang of disappointment. I am so eager to jump into this new life.

Pete points out the unclaimed bed in a front room. A framed photograph and a hairbrush sit on the bureau; a large mustard-colored suitcase fills the space at the foot of the other bed. My roommate must be a minimalist.

"I'll let you get settled," Pete says. "Come on, Stella, it's bedtime. We'll see you tomorrow, Nola."

Stella turns and waves to me, curling each finger down one at a time.

"There's a staff meeting right after breakfast," Pete shouts from the bottom of the stairs, and then he is gone.

I'm left standing in the dim room. The mattress on my cot is musty and stained, the feather pillow looks as if it went flat somewhere around the sixties. I throw on a sweatshirt and spread out my sleeping bag, but I don't unpack my duffel, though two open drawers have clearly been reserved for me.

I flop down on the bed and stare up at the faded graffiti on the ceiling. *Barb loves Tom. Nancy will never forget Don.* The girls' names are so old-fashioned, I suddenly feel surrounded by ghosts. And where do the guys come from? Waiters? Maintenance? Guests, maybe.

Then it happens, as it often does at this time of day. My best buddies, Fear and Doubt, locked arm in arm, close in. I'm suddenly so afraid of my decision. So afraid of my own selfishness.

How I wish I were back in my living room cajoling Song to eat something.

I pull out my phone to call home.

No answer.

Chapter 4

Hey, Song—

Sorry I missed ya when I called this morning. How was your appointment? I was going to e-mail but found this periwinkle on the beach and wanted to send it. Remember Gotts Island? You found the tiniest periwinkle any of us had ever seen. This one may not be tiny, but it still reminds me of you. (I hope it didn't get crushed in the envelope!)

After a quick run on Rocky Cove's dirt roads, I checked out the shore. Eggemoggin Reach is gorgeous! Fog made the pine trees and islands look so painterly. The water was gray silk.

Enough about the scenery. I know you want the skinny. There are five other waitresses. Four of them are also from out of state and have worked here other summers; my roommate is a local girl who went home for the weekend, so I haven't met her yet. I'm guessing, from a picture on her bureau, that she has a boyfriend. The alpha girls are Lucy (head waitress and hostess) and Brita. Lucy is that perfect combination of smart and pretty. (Don't ask me how I can tell she's smart—maybe she ate her French toast in an extremely intelligent way.) Brita has eyes that are almost black, long dark curly hair, and should be in a French film. The other two are Annie and Mariah, and they seem nice enough. I thought there might be more girls— chambermaids, maybe—but Pete hires women from town to do the housekeeping.

Will, unbelievably hot maintenance guy, has a thing for Lucy. (Too bad.) As far as I can tell, there are only five guys: two other maintenance guys (waaay immature); Kevin, who is kitchen help; and Nigel, the "rec director," who takes his job very seriously. Cute but . . . (that's "but" with one "t").

I should go. We're about to begin a first-aid course (in case guests in the dining room choke on a bone or, worse, have a heart attack). After that, I'm taking Pete's daughter, Stella, swimming. Her mother, Susanna, is running around like a maniac trying to prepare for opening day, so I offered.

Here's your haiku (see, I kept my promise):

> Dreaded decisions
> Are thoroughly confused by
> Magical thinking

Love ya lots,

Nola

I try not to feel like a tagalong as I follow the other girls to the staff meeting. They're talking in code, the way old friends do when entering familiar territory. *It won't be long before you know the inside stuff too,* I pep talk myself.

Soon after the meeting starts (this part should be titled "Pete's List of Don'ts": Don't swim on the guest beach or even consider jumping into the ocean from the ledges; Don't linger in the main office; Don't take food from the kitchen; Don't for one moment think that any of the equipment, recreational opportunities, or luxuries offered here are for YOU), my roommate arrives and sits as close to the door as possible. She appears to be studying her thumbnail, the knotty pine walls, the pattern on her Crocs.

What she doesn't do is make eye contact with anyone in the room.

The instructor tells us to find a first-aid partner. I watch the easy, automatic pairing of the other waitresses and then walk over and introduce myself to my roommate, whose name turns out to be Bridget, and help her tie a tourniquet around my arm. She keeps her head down—her hair over her eyes—trying to listen to the directions. Every now and then I point or mumble something ("This way, I think") to redirect her, and as she fumbles with the strip of bedsheet, I realize that maybe she isn't so tough, maybe she's just shy. She relaxes a little and gives me a nod just as the class is ending. So I feel bad when bikini-clad Stella calls me from the porch, a green pail and shovel in one hand and pink sunglasses in the other.

"I promised I'd take her swimming," I explain, and then wish, as the two of us walk up the road, along a dirt path past Robin Hood Camp for Boys and down to a sandy beach, that I'd thought to ask Bridget if she'd like to come too. It's been so long since I've just hung out with friends, I guess I've forgotten how to act.

Stella gives me a brief tour of a little hut containing fishing gear, life jackets, beach chairs, and sand toys. She points out the rowboats, a canoe, and kayaks lining the tree line.

"Hi, Harrison," she yells when she reaches the water's edge.

I come nearer to see who she is talking to. A dog? An imaginary lake creature?

She points to some docks to the right of the beach. A bare-chested guy with longish, sandy brown hair walks up to shore, easily lifts a small sailboat, and carries it down to the water. He maneuvers the boat alongside the dock and then crouches to tie it in place.

Up he goes for the next boat. "Hey, Stella!" he calls, without breaking his rhythm.

Ah, so maybe it's to Robin Hood that the others travel at night.

"Who's that?" I whisper.

Stella looks up at me. "Har-ri-son."

I add the *duh* in my mind and surprise her by being the first to run and dive into the icy lake water. It takes my breath away, and I come up with a whoop.

Stella laughs and then, with surprising courage, does the same.

Knowing that we're being watched prevents me from racing back to shore as quickly as I can. I swim in a circle, keeping my eye on Stella until I get used to the water temperature. Then I stand and encourage her to dog-paddle toward me. The sandy bottom feels soft but clear of muck. After swinging Stella motorboat-fashion until my shoulders ache, then having a few underwater tea parties, I look to see if Harrison is still tying knots.

He's nowhere in sight.

chapter 5

At the barn I find Bridget stretched out on her bed, staring at the ceiling. She's been crying.

"You okay?" I ask.

She sniffs.

I look around the room for something to offer her—a tissue, a glass of water—but can find nothing. "Would you like me to go down to the inn, get you a soda from the machine?"

"Better not," she mutters.

"There's diet, I think. There might even be water."

"All right," she says.

"Which?"

She just looks at me.

"What do you want?"

"To get the hell out of here!" she says, bursting into tears again.

I sit down on the end of her creaky cot and wait. It's

something I've seen nurses do with Song. They seem to know that the best way to encourage someone to spill is to simply show up. Be here. So that's what I do . . . and Bridget begins to talk.

There is Sam—a guy her parents hate. Not only is Sam three years older than she is, but he's gone from job to job in his years since high school. Her parents made her apply to Rocky Cove in an attempt to separate them. "But I'm not going to let them do that," Bridget cries. "Sam came and got me Friday, and we spent the weekend at his family's camp."

"Sounds as if he really wants to be with you," I say.

"Don't know if he'll feel that way six months from now." She pauses.

I wait.

"I'm pregnant," she says.

Yikes. "Does Sam know?" I whisper.

She shakes her head.

"Your parents?"

"God, no! They'd disown me."

"What are you going to do?"

"I haven't decided." Bridget sniffs.

I scoot into the tiny bathroom and pull some toilet paper off the roll. "Can Sam help you?" I ask, handing Bridget the

TP. The room across from ours is empty, but giggles bounce off the walls in Lucy's room.

"You see," says Bridget, wiping her nose, "there's another girl in town pregnant with Sam's baby too."

Staff training that afternoon is a relief. We all have to learn housekeeping techniques in case the chambermaids need help during peak season. I can figure out what to do with the corners of the stiff, bleached sheets, but what to do about Bridget?

It's not that I'm incapable of sympathizing. I suppose, if I were leading another life, I could imagine myself getting caught up in the moment and ending up pregnant. *Will she need my care?*

And the fact that there is another girl in town pregnant by Sam—well, that part seems a little sketchy.

And really lousy, I admit.

"The blankets should be so tight," the housekeeper is saying, "so tight that you can throw a nickel on the surface and the coin will bounce."

She throws the nickel. It doesn't bounce—it just sits there. She shrugs. "Tight enough," she says, getting a laugh from all of us.

"Nola!" says Susanna as I come down the inn stairs,

having learned the proper way to shine a bathroom faucet, make a sailboat out of a hand towel, and get beach sand out of the area rugs. "I was wondering if you might be available for babysitting tonight?"

Ah. She can read my sign: DULL LIFE, BUT GOOD WITH KIDS.

"Pete and I are hoping to go into Ellsworth and see a play at the Grand. Stella specifically asked for you."

Well, what are my options? My mind searches for an excuse. I could say I'm hoping to spend some time getting to know the other waitresses, but we both know I have all summer to do that.

"I promise we won't impose on you after this," she says. "Stella's regular babysitter arrives in a couple days."

"Sure," I say. "What time should I come over?"

"Well," Susanna says rather sheepishly. "Stella's having an early dinner in the kitchen. How about now?"

As I pick at the ignored french fries on her plate, I wonder if I'm being paid extra for this. I should have said, *Sure, I charge ten dollars an hour.* That would have been professional. Or, *Will you just add the hours to my paycheck?* For some reason, Carly, the girl on the bus, pops into my head. She would have known how to handle it. Immediately, I'm defending Susanna to the likes of Carly Whitehouse—

explaining that she did seem to get that it was imposing.

When Stella is in bed, I walk around the Lovells' apartment on the third floor of the inn. It's old—the floors are more beat up than in the guest rooms, and the braided rugs have obviously been in the family for a long time. I pull away the lace curtains on one window, but it's too dark to see anything. I wonder if the other waitresses are hanging in the barn or if they've gone out again. Wonder if anyone is seeing Har-ri-son. I close my eyes and imagine myself flying out the window and into the night.

chapter 6

Still half asleep, I hear Bridget stagger back to bed. "You okay?"

"I'm so sick of puking, or feeling like I have to."

"What time is it?"

"I think six. I'm really sorry."

I push down my irritation. "Don't be sorry," I say. "I always get up early. Besides, we have to be at breakfast soon."

"Ugh. There is no way I can do breakfast." She turns over, faces the wall.

"I know, you need saltines!" What Song eats whenever she's nauseous. "I'll bring some back for you."

Bridget sits up, looks at me. "Sorry I'm such a drag. I used to be fun once upon a time."

"Yeah, sure," I say. "Likely story."

She almost laughs.

I'm too early for breakfast. The chef is singing in the kitchen, so I poke my head in. He and one of the kitchen helpers are slicing up veggies for omelets. "Don't even think about it," he says.

"Excuse me?" I ask.

"Hanging around here between meals."

I flush. "Sorry," I say. "I haven't figured——"

"You're Nola," he says.

I step forward, hoping he's only gruff on the outside.

"And I'm Cheffie. Consider yourself introduced."

No. He *is* gruff——and into giving the new girl a hard time.

I'm about to leave when Kevin, maybe a year or two older than me, with bed head and morning stubble, signals me into the dishwashing area. The entire space is stainless steel: silver dishwashing machine, silver counters, silver sinks, silver spray hose. The guy is sitting up on a stool eating a crepe.

"Want a bite?" he asks.

I shake my head.

"Don't worry about him. He's always like this first thing in the morning. So you're Nola?"

I nod. *How does he know my name?*

"Trust me, it won't take you long to figure things out. My third summer."

"You must like it—here, I mean—if you're back for a third time."

He holds out his hand for me to shake. "Meet the world's next great chef," he says. "I get lots of experience in this kitchen." He lowers his voice. "Though they still won't let me cover on his"—he nods to the wall—"day off."

"Have you washed those pots yet, Kevin?" Cheffie calls out.

Kevin smirks. He doesn't seem worried about Cheffie's snap, but it scares me. Like some little kid.

Still needing to kill time, I go into the reception area and poke around. There's a table with gifts for sale: postcards of Eggemoggin Reach, pillows stuffed with sweet-smelling pine needles, lobster trap Christmas ornaments, and blueberry jam. Mom loves jam. Maybe I'll send her some.

On another wall, behind the desk, I see a copy machine and, above it, wooden mailboxes. Do I have one? Sure enough, there's a box with my name on it (cool) and inside is a number and a phone message . . . from Carly Whitehouse!

I choose one of the rockers on the porch—as far from the doors and other ears as possible—and call her. Mariah and Annie are walking down the hill to breakfast, and for a moment I think of joining them, but I have already dialed Carly's number and can't wait to hear her voice. It isn't till I hear the ring tone that I think of the time. *Ack. I have the social IQ of a gnat.*

"Oh, sorry, sorry, sorry. Did I wake you up?" I ask when I hear Carly's groggy voice on the other end of the line.

"Nola," she says, coming to. "How's the high life?"

"Ha!" I sputter. "If you call hanging with Stella the high life, then just fine."

"Ah. Stella Bella. What about the other waitresses? They around yet? Are they nice?"

"They're here, but I haven't really had a chance . . . I have a roommate, but she's, well, depressed."

"Depressed?"

"She's in love and pregnant."

There's a pause. "Does Pete know?"

"I'm pretty sure he doesn't. How are *you*, foster sister? You staying in Bangor for a while?" If Carly says yes, I will *definitely* figure out some way to meet her on my day off.

From: Nola
To: Song
Subject: From the servant's quarters

Song,

I've sent you a letter but wanted to shoot you an
e-mail as well. Here's what I learned this morning:

1) The perfect table setting includes three plates, two
   glasses, and six types of silverware.

2) Stains on white tablecloths are covered by white
   linen napkins called "nappies."

3) Orders are never written down until the waitress
   reaches the kitchen.

4) Uniforms are baby blue with navy, frilly aprons.
   (Stop laughing.)

There's the glamour you imagined. Guests start
arriving the day after tomorrow. Hope I'm ready.

Two new waitresses
Add four more who know their stuff
Trays bound to collide

<3

Nola

I don't tell Song that the other waitresses spent most
of the dining room training reminiscing about past years.
Their stories were funny, but I was drowning. Which side
of the person do you serve on? Do I remove the salad
plate and the bread plate after the first course? How am

I going to figure everything out in two days?

I tried to talk to Mariah when Lucy went to get the xylophone we use to call the guests to dinner (we all have to play the same traditional tune when it's our turn to sound the chimes). "So do you find it hard? Keeping all of this in your head, I mean?" She just shrugged.

Nor do I tell Song that after talking briefly with Pete, I find myself alone in the barn, having no idea where the others are—Bridget included. So I do what I've always done when I'm edgy or aggravated. I put on my trainers and run.

Instead of exploring more of the Rocky Cove paths, I take the town road away from the inn and its complicated history. It's really beat up—a narrow winding strip of cracked pavement and potholes. Beyond the driveway that leads to the lake beach and the camp, there is mostly field and forest and, scattered here and there, a few houses (presumably with lake or ocean views, depending on which side of the road you're on). My chest is tight, my rhythm off—not my usual form. I can't help it. I feel so . . . what? So thinly present, nothing more than a wisp of substance— like the fog that clings to the early Maine daylight. I push harder against the sea breeze.

I should be used to being an outsider. Having a sister with cancer has turned me into a freak show. Kids know me as "Nolaherlittlesisterhasabraintumor." I seem to walk with an extra-long shadow—the shadow of what may come. When I'm finally noticed for something at school—a decent poem in the *Gazette* or for breaking a cross-country record—I swear I can hear the words *You know, she's the one . . .*

Tumors scare others—even adults. It's as if they think they can catch Song's disease from me. Or when they look at me, they don't know what to say—as if talking to me requires the exact right words—so they don't say anything. I don't blame them, not really. I probably wouldn't say anything to me either.

I speed up, getting into a hard sprint up not one, but two steep hills. When I reach the second peak, I slow down enough to notice a rocky, rooty footpath on the left. *Why not?* I think. What I don't anticipate is the view awaiting me.

No fog at this time of day. Eggemoggin Reach flickers with flames of light, islands rise from the sea.

"Wow," I say aloud.

"Pretty amazing, huh?"

God, he scared me! It's Harrison. He's sitting on a rock, knees folded up, a backpack at his feet. "Welcome to Lookout Hill. Peanut butter sandwich?" he asks, holding out half.

Two guys offering me food in the same day!

"I'm good," I say, out of breath—from the run, of course. "I was curious about this path—where it would lead."

"All the paths lead to some kind of water around here. If not the ocean or a lake, some local watering hole. You discovered the path to Hostess House?"

"What's that?"

"A cabin on the edge of Robin Hood. Lots of us meet there at night."

"Hard to believe there's any place to hang out." Do I sound citified? Critical? I don't mean to be. Rocky Cove is beautiful. Remote, but beautiful. I wish I'd said something a little more gracious.

"Oh, there are some fun places—you'll see," Harrison says. "You're the girl I saw with Stella the other day, right?"

I nod, stretching my quads in a lunge. My heart gives a quick pop. I've been remembered!

"Babysitter?"

"Oh, no," I say, a little emphatically, I guess. "Waitress." God, I sound ridiculous, as if the title of waitress somehow has more prestige. "But I have no idea what I'm doing," I quickly add.

"I'm sure you'll figure it out."

Worse than ridiculous—stupid. "Season opens day after tomorrow." I start to bend my torso from one side to the other, but catch myself before acting like a total stretching fool. "How about camp? Do you have campers yet?"

"Same as you. Two days to go."

"You a counselor?"

"Waterfront director." He gets up and walks over to me. "Here. Do you know the names of the islands?"

"Well, I know one is Pumpkin and another is Deer Isle." Song and I had pored over the website map, giving us both something to imagine (until she realized I was serious about going). He's standing close enough for me to read the tiny words FLICK OFF on his gray T-shirt.

"Well, that's Pumpkin," he says. He smells of peanut butter, sunscreen, and lake. I take a slow, even breath to grab these scents away from the salt air.

"But you can't see Deer Isle from here," he says. "It's off in that direction." He points over the tree line.

"Shows what I know. So what's the name of *that* one?" I point to a seemingly floating cluster of trees.

"Can't remember. I was hoping you knew."

"Nope. But I can teach you how to fold a napkin four different ways."

"Cool," he says, and laughs.

"Um . . . did you run here too?"

"Nah. I'm more of a Taoist. You know, live the effortless life." His eyes laugh. "I walk, I sail, I sleep."

"You eat peanut butter sandwiches."

"Easier than a BLT."

I smile and try to think of something witty or otherwise interesting to say.

"Well, have a good run," he says, turning.

"You too. I mean . . . a good walk."

Harrison gives a little nod and heads down the same path I came on.

When I get back to the barn, Bridget is coming out, mustard suitcase in hand. There's a car idling out front.

"Hey, you're leaving?" I ask.

"As if you didn't know," she says.

"What?"

There's someone in the front seat of the car, but he's staying right where he is. I reach out to help Bridget lift her suitcase.

"Get away," she snaps.

For a moment I imagine she has heard my deepest thoughts about her. "Bridget, talk to me," I say, trying to get her to look me in the eye.

She throws her suitcase into the trunk, slams it shut, and climbs into the car.

I step back, and she rolls away without another word or a wave.

Chapter 7

When I walk into the staff dining room for dinner, I'm startled. It's completely empty. I check my watch, but I'm not early.

I'm about to turn and leave as Nigel comes in. Standing there by myself, I feel naked. I think I'll pretend that I've just finished, that I'm heading up to the barn, but he asks how my day was as he hands me a plate and so I serve myself from the buffet.

When we sit down, I expect him to say, *Where is everyone?* But he doesn't and I'm relieved. It would be embarrassing to tell him that I have no idea.

But then, Nigel seems perfectly content alone. In fact, even when we're all together, Nigel seems . . . apart. When he's not writing on scraps of paper (to-do lists? observations? philosophical musings?), he's got his nose in a book. He appears to be considering something knotty and complex all the time. But the minute you open your mouth, he stops and looks at you with this intensely curious expression—like he just woke up, and there you are—and now there's nothing more he'd like to do than listen to what you have to say. It's sweet.

So I immediately ask about Bridget—does he know what's happened? But he doesn't. He tells me that every year one or two of the new waitresses don't work out and that it's not unheard of for local help to bail even before the season begins. There's an invisible line between the locals and those "from away," and not everyone is comfortable crossing it. But that doesn't explain her rudeness to me. I don't know how to say this without sounding like a drama queen, so I don't.

"So what made you apply here?" he asks.

There's a part of me that would like to tell him the truth. That I couldn't spend any more time talking about white blood cell counts. That I had a wild and determined fantasy of experiencing a scrapbook teen experience in just one summer—a sort of makeup course. But I don't know him yet. "Thought I should start earning for college," I say. "And coming to Maine seemed like fun. How about you?"

He looks down. "Family tradition," he says, and I'm not sure what that means. Would he have been more honest—more revealing—if I had been?

He tells me stories about past summers: the pain of learning to water-ski, having to coordinate and lead ridiculously competitive bocce tournaments, performing talent shows for the guests. And then, as if his stories were boring me, he quietly informs me of other staff events: diving off the forbidden ledges, playing pranks on the chef, breaking curfew to sleep out under the stars. It sounds as if he knows of these activities but isn't a part of them. I hope it won't be the same for me.

Finally, it's time to head back to the barn. It's starting to get dark, and the night is eerily quiet. Nigel's cabin is in the opposite direction, but he offers to walk me up.

I start to accept but stop myself. "Thanks," I say. "I'm okay."

"You sure?"

I nod. A question had occurred to me while I was listening to Nigel. If I *did* have the chance to jump off some ledge into the sea, would I?

Maybe I'll start by being brave enough to walk back through the Maine woods at night by myself. I jog off down the dirt road and then slow. Walking outside suddenly seems much easier than entering the empty barn, going through the storage shed, and up the dark narrow stairs.

I feel my way into my dim room, and before I can register the face, I register a body. I'm all alone in this doorway, and there's someone here waiting for me. I turn to run back downstairs.

"Hey," a familiar voice yells.

"Oh my God!" I scream. "What are you doing here?"

"Say hi to the new Rocky Cove waitress," Carly says.

Apparently, Pete called her as soon as he found out Bridget was leaving. I jump up and down and hug her. I can't believe my luck. What are the chances of meeting someone on a bus and having her turn out to be your roommate? Maybe events aren't random.

Mariah walks into the room with a grocery bag in hand. "What's going on?" she asks.

"Carly here is taking Bridget's place."

"You know each other?" asks Lucy, popping in as well. Brita and Annie follow her.

I open my mouth to explain, but Carly just says, "We are the *best* of friends."

I look at her, wanting so much for it to be true.

"Looks like you've been party shopping," she says to Mariah. "When's the event?"

"How did you know?" Annie asks.

"At what other time do we socialites carry full bags of groceries?"

"Where are you from, Carly?" Lucy asks.

"Boston."

I expected Carly to say Bangor. But then, she has two homes, doesn't she? And I suppose Boston is more impressive than a small city in Maine.

"What part?" Brita asks.

"Beacon Hill."

"My aunt used to live on Beacon Hill," Annie says. "I bet we know someone in common."

"Michael Walden?" Carly asks.

"Yes!" Annie shouts. "I can't believe that. You know Michael? He's so hot."

"And so—"

"Wealthy," says Annie.

"As rich as Yacht Guy?" I interject. Carly had mentioned this guy on the bus, and I'm suddenly afraid that she has more in common with the others than with me.

"Not sure," says Carly. "It's hard to know the depth of a trust fund."

The others laugh.

"We better get going," Mariah says.

"Join us," says Lucy. "You and Nola. We're having a party down at Flatlanders Beach."

"Wouldn't miss it," Carly says. "Would we, Nola?"

"We wouldn't," I say, knowing that everything from now on will be different here.

Chapter 8

On the way to Flatlanders, I think about how Dad always talks of life changing gradually, but that hasn't been my experience at all. If you ask me, life takes wild, unexpected turns. Like Carly.

"What's up?" she says from behind me. Under one arm she's carrying sticks she's gathered. She drapes the other arm around my shoulder.

"Life at Rocky Cove," I say.

We have just come into view of the reach, and even though the sun's set on the lake side of the property, the ocean has taken on an amazing glow.

"Okay. Let me see if I've got it." A gentle pressure on my arm gives me the message to slow down and listen as the others walk quietly ahead down the dirt road past the cabins and eventually off Rocky Cove property to a beach that is apparently owned by Nigel's grandmother. Oh, family tradition.

"I've got the waitresses," Carly goes on, pointing to them and whispering their names. "And I know who Nigel is—he's the future owner of this place."

"How do you know about Nigel?" I ask.

Carly shakes her head. "I don't know anything about Nigel. He just behaves in ways that tell me he has lots of influence."

"Like deciding when to have a bingo tournament. Big decisions like that?"

"Go ahead and laugh, but you'll see what I mean before the summer is over."

Mariah drops back. "Be careful with that bag," she says to me. "You have very important supplies."

"What?" Carly asks.

"Bottle of wine," I sing softly.

"Fruit of the vine," Carly joins in. *"When you gonna let me get sober?"*

"I can't believe it! You know that song!" I cry, hoping we're far enough from the inn not to be heard.

"So you guys grew up together, eh? In a bar?" says Annie.

"Maybe we did," Carly says. "No doubt our moms downed a few before we were born."

I'm about to say that my mother wouldn't be caught

dead in a bar but stop myself. Let them think my life is anything but boring.

Carly whoops. We've arrived at a cliff above Flatlanders Beach. A small cottage seems to grow out of the ledge.

"Amazing, huh?" Carly runs down the hill, drops her pile of wood near an open fire pit, peels down to her tank top and boy shorts, and dives into the water.

"How can she do that?" shrieks Annie.

"I don't know, but it looks like fun!" Kevin strips down to his boxers and plunges in after her.

"Well, damn," says Will, taking the challenge.

"Come on, Nola Granola," Carly shouts. "Don't tell me you can't swim."

I lower the bag I've been carrying, taking a quick mental check of what I put on after my shower. Sports bra, that's good. Am I the type to run across the beach in my underwear? Why not?

The water's freezing—so much more so than the icy lake—but exhilarating.

Kevin, Will, and Brita don't last a minute.

"Come on!" Carly dares me out to a buoy and back. We swim with swift strokes, matching each other in strength and speed. Reaching the buoy together is like crossing the finish line simultaneously with your cross-country running mates.

"So, shall we keep going to Pumpkin Island out there?" Carly asks.

She'd better be kidding. "I will if you will," I say.

Carly looks out at sea, then turns back with a "You know, that wine would taste pretty good now too."

I nod. I don't drink, or at least I haven't up till now, but I'm definitely grateful we're not swimming farther out to sea.

Annie waits on shore with a pile of beach towels she grabbed from the cabana hut as we passed the guests' beach. Shivering, I take the top one. Carly digs down until she finds a towel with Minnie Mouse posing for a camera and wraps it around her shoulders. Then she walks toward a newly crackling fire to see who else has arrived.

"Want me to get your clothes?" Kevin asks me.

I glance around. My stuff is scattered among the feet of guys who seem to have appeared from nowhere.

"Robin Hood counselors?" I ask.

"Yup." He seems slightly amused, the kind of kid who would combine all his pet lizards—male and female—just to see what they would do.

I retreat behind him and scan the scene. God, there

he is! Harrison is at this party. I feel heat rise up into my ears.

"I'll take this hiding behind me as a yes . . . about your clothes," says Kevin.

"What?"

"Wait here." A minute later he's back with my jeans and sweatshirt.

"Nola," says Carly as I approach the fire, running my fingers through my hair, hoping I don't look like some half-drowned mutt. "This is Dominic," she says, pointing. "He's from Columbia."

"The school, not the country," adds one of the other guys.

Dominic says, "I'm the trip counselor."

"And this is Harrison, right?" says Carly, placing her hand on his arm.

Harrison waves a bottle at me as a sort of hello again, but in no other way indicates that we've already met. He turns to Carly. "And who are you?"

"Carly Whitehouse," says Dominic. "Right?"

"Wow! Good memory," says Carly. "I'll quiz you later," she says to Harrison, giving his arm a squeeze.

"Are these get-togethers regular events?" I ask Kevin as I button my jeans.

"Not really. Last summer the girls didn't get up the nerve till mid-August. I guess this year they're not wasting any time."

Despite Carly's energetic round of introductions, the beach party is still in this awkward, "what now?" stage. Brita and Mariah simultaneously look to Lucy as if to say, *You're better at this than we are—do something.* But Lucy couldn't care less whether the Rocky-Cove-meets-Robin-Hood affair is a success. She's already sitting on a piece of driftwood, bare legs stretched in front of her, chatting with Will. He doesn't seem to give two hoots about the others either.

"We have a ton of food here," Mariah says. "Anyone want a pork rind?" She holds out the package, but only Kevin is a taker.

"These are disgusting!" he says after one taste. "If you'd given me some advance warning, I could have cooked up something spectacular."

The night grows cooler, we huddle closer to the fire, and the talk ceases again.

Carly pulls me away. "Let's do something to liven things up."

"Like what?" I say.

"We'll put on a skit."

"Playacting?" I think of Song and all the skits we've put on for my parents. But those performances never said "beach party" to me.

"Oh, come on. We want people to loosen up. Help me find a stick. A long one. Trust me."

We climb back up the hill and into the woods to find the stick that Carly has in mind. During that time, she tells me my lines.

"I don't get it," I say. "We pretend the stick is a candy store counter and I ask you if you have these certain types of candy. And that's funny how?"

"I told you to trust me," says Carly. "It'll be funny."

Dragging the stick back toward camp, I look around to see if anyone's noticed we've been missing.

"More firewood?" asks Nigel.

"I wish," I say with a laugh.

Carly wastes no time telling the others that she and I are going to put on a performance and that she needs two male volunteers to hold each end of the stick.

Awkward smiles all around. Finally, Harrison and Dominic volunteer.

Carly pretends to be a candy store clerk. Even Lucy and Will have stopped talking to watch.

"Do you have any Sugar Babies?" I, the customer, ask.

Carly glances at the two guys at the ends of the pole and says, "Nope, no Sugar Babies."

"How about some Red Hots?"

Again, Carly glances at each of the guys. "No. No Red Hots, either."

A few of the waitresses and counselors giggle. It is a nervous laugh, but it makes me think this idea might not be so bad after all.

"How about Tootsies? SweeTarts?"

Carly shakes her head sadly.

"Whoppers?"

Carly gives each of the guys a long, contemplative glance, then an exaggerated frown.

The guys crack up.

"Well," I say in an exasperated voice (I'm getting into my part now), "what *do* you have?"

Carly looks to her left and her right. She slows down and delivers the punch line: "Just two suckers on a stick."

Real laughter from the others this time.

"Yeah, Dum-Dums," shouts one of them.

Carly looks at me, her eyes saying one thing: *Told you so.*

chapter 9

After our last first aid class the next day, Mariah suggests we all pile into her old Volvo wagon and head for the Gull's Nest.

"It's a gift shop," Annie explains.

Carly says, "Let me grab my millions."

The gift shop is all things nautical. "Look at this string of starfish lights, Nolie, and this seashell mobile." Carly dances around the shop pointing out treasure after treasure.

I'm wondering whether I should buy a second beach towel with my birthday money when she suggests we decorate our room to look like a mermaid's den.

"We can get Mariah to take us to a hardware store and buy sea green paint. Then we'd hang these lights and a couple of mobiles, and look, Nol, look at this coral rug!"

"You think Pete will let us paint the walls?" I ask.

"Why not? There's nothing but graffiti on them now. We'll paint the walls *and* the ceiling!"

I can barely lift my fork that night at dinner. I hope the paint will come off my fingers before our first night of waitressing.

Stella slides off her seat (where and when did Pete and Susanna eat?) and comes over to me. She touches her hand to my wrist and asks, "Will you play croquet with me?"

A wishbone pulled in two directions, I smile at Stella. I look up to see if others can be coerced into a game. No takers.

"I have an even better idea than croquet," says Carly. "Stella, have you ever seen a mermaid's den?"

I sigh gratefully.

That night not only does Stella get permission to come upstairs in the barn (which is normally off-limits to boys, children, and guests), but so do Nigel, Will, and the rest of the help. Kevin brings a blender and makes batches of "seaweed smoothies," which taste a lot like blueberry banana. Will docks his iPod, and Jimmy Buffett tunes fill the room. Carly and Stella do a mermaid dance to "Margaritaville." Then Stella lies down on my cot (twisting among the bodies seated there) and puts her head on my lap. I run my fingers through her hair, and when I stop briefly, she looks up at me and says, "More."

Carly scoots onto the bed and puts her head in my lap too.

Nigel, with camera strung around his neck tonight, starts to take our picture. But then he slowly lowers the lens from his face.

"What?" asks Carly.

"I don't know," he says. "Suddenly, I feel like I've met you before."

Chapter 10

From: Song
To: Nola
Subject: Landlocked

Hey, Nola—

Thanks for the periwinkle! It arrived in one piece.
Send me more sea treasures—and letters. I like
getting something in the mail. I like seeing your
horrible handwriting. Besides, you sound like you're
actually talking to ME when you write letters.

The last chemo wasn't that bad, which is good news
and bad news. The good news is that I felt like doing
things with Mom after. The bad news is that I never
think it's working when I don't feel awful.

You would think she would
Dream of running or flying
She dreams of needles

Write back SOON.

xo

Song

I hit reply, but realize I don't have time to respond to Song now, so I close out. I have to get to the dining hall for dinner. I wolf down Cheffie's shepherd's pie and take my place to greet the guests. It's our third night of waitressing, and Lucy tells me I'll have more than a few tables now, but I think I'm ready.

My first two tables: Mrs. Barnes, a woman in her seventies who has come here for generations, and the Winstons, a family of six, who will be my guests for the whole summer. On top of them, I'm assigned "transients"—a couple who made a reservation to eat here at the inn but have their own summer home nearby. Apparently, they come often and immediately identify me as new. "Seems we're always training someone," the man mutters. His wife gives me a "don't mind him" smile. The pressure is on.

Next I'm assigned a family who arrived this afternoon: parents with a girl about Song's age and her best friend. The girls are both wearing strapless dresses and adorable shoes. I have to say hello quickly—I'm moving from table to table trying to remember the sequence: drinks, rolls, pickle tray, order, appetizers, salad . . . what I have or haven't done so far.

It's harder than I expected. For some reason, Mrs.

Barnes wants to gab tonight. I approach her table with her V8 juice, and she holds my arm. "Do you ever have difficulty sleeping, Nola? Last night I was awake from two o'clock on. There's a great horned owl on the property, and usually, I enjoy their call, but last night . . ."

I like Mrs. Barnes. She seems rugged for a seventy-year-old, but tonight she's making me nervous. I should tell her I have to keep moving, but it feels mean—like I'm dismissing her.

"Nola!" one of the youngest Winstons calls out from the family dining room. Yikes.

"Oh no," says Mrs. Barnes. "I forgot to ask you for a tall glass, dear. You see, my doctor has prescribed two and a half cups of fruits and vegetables a day. Can you imagine?"

"That's okay," I say. "I'll get you a tall glass."

"Nola," whispers Lucy, passing by, "Mr. Winston wants another basket of rolls and has decided to have his steak rare instead of medium rare."

I nod. "I'll be right back with that V8, Mrs. Barnes."

"Oh, and don't let me forget to tell you about my dream. . . ."

I run to the kitchen, dump the juice into a large glass, and top it off. Next I pull the Winston order off the clothesline above the chef's table, cross out the *MR* and write in *R*.

"Hey!" Cheffie bellows. "If you're going to make a change like that, you better tell me. How do you know I'll look at the order again?"

"Next time I will," I yell as I head back out to the porch dining room, placing the juice on Mrs. Barnes's table from behind so no eye contact is made, and then hurry to the family dining room to pick up the Winstons' bread basket.

"Nola," says the man who is dining for the evening, "could we have our salads, please?"

I had totally forgotten them in the corner.

I can't seem to get all the balls in the air. One timing mistake leads to another and then to another. I mistakenly pocket Mrs. Barnes's dinner order; the shoe girls' mashed potatoes are cold. I'm taking the plates back to the kitchen when Pete pulls me over to say, "I stopped by the Winston table. They thought their waitress had vanished."

"I'm sorry," I mumble, and duck into the dishwashing area before bursting into tears.

Kevin stops spraying and comes around the dirty-dish counter.

"I have no idea what I'm doing," I sputter.

I think he's going to give me a hug, but he turns me around and steers me into the little pantry where box lunches are made. He seems calm despite the fact we've both gone AWOL. If Pete walks in, I'll be fired on the spot.

"Here is your arsenal of secret weapons," he says, opening a refrigerator. "This is mint from the garden—bring it to those who order tea."

"V8 juice?"

"That will work too." He continues, "This is maple butter—bring it to anyone who orders the baked apples for dessert."

"Why don't we always serve maple butter?"

"Shhh. This is gold. Got kids at your table?" He reaches up and pulls out a bag of miniature marshmallows. "Put these on their ice cream."

"Won't I get in trouble?"

"Not if you let guests know that these treats are for *them* and *them only*."

He's right. For the rest of the night I come bearing secret gifts, and all prior sins are forgotten.

Just the same, I can't get Pete's words out of my head. I wonder if he's having serious doubts about me, and I realize at that moment that I really, really want to stay.

On my way up to my room later, I stop at the computer to respond to Song. I keep it short:

From: Nola
To: Song
Subject: Quick reply

Hey, Song,

Okay, I'll write more letters. Just finished serving
dinner. I totally suck as a waitress. It's so much
harder than I thought. If I don't improve, I'll be back
listening to your alternative music before you know
it. Hey, did Mom tell you that I met a girl on the bus,
Carly Whitehouse, and now we're roommates?!

Cinderella shoes
Sparkle on others tonight
I'm sweeping ashes

Love,

Me

I step over Carly, who is sitting in our doorway talking
to Annie, who is sitting in her doorway, and pull out my
running clothes.

"You're going for a run *now*? Why? What's wrong?"
Carly asks.

"I just had the evening from hell, that's what's wrong."

"But we're going into Blue Hill. Will knows about a
party at one of the summer homes."

"I don't think so," I say. "I'm really not in the mood."

"Oh, come on," Carly says.

"I just couldn't pull it all together tonight."

"Is that why you're spending the summer in Maine?"

"Excuse me?"

"To be the best *waitress* you can be?"

I have to laugh.

"Come on, Nolie, you came for the social life. Now get dressed."

I obediently change into a jean skirt and flip-flops. Carly puts on a vintage lace dress with tie-up sandals, and we join the others, who are dividing themselves among Mariah's and Nigel's cars.

"Nola Granola and I will sit in the little seat in the back of the Volvo," Carly announces.

"No making out back there," Kevin shouts.

I shoot him a "don't even think of going there" look, but Carly says, "Kevin, you ruin all the fun."

Chapter 11

I've never crashed a party before (surprise, surprise) and can't help feeling that I'm wearing a giant NOT INVITED sign. *You're only here for the summer,* I tell myself. *If we're all kicked out of this house, no harm done—we still have one another.*

I follow Carly's lead and take a beer from a cooler, then follow her through a sea of bodies to the back deck.

"Hey!" someone calls through the screen door. It's Dominic and, beside him, Harrison. My breath catches. What is it about this guy? He's said only a dozen words to me, but there's something about him that makes my insides want to come out and play. I say hello to Dominic and wait nervously for Harrison to acknowledge me, but he seems fully engaged in a conversation with a guy I don't recognize.

"Hear you had a rough evening." It's Nigel behind me.

"How'd you hear?" I ask, flipping around.

"Lucy said."

I quickly translate: Lucy told Will, Nigel, and Annie—all those who had driven over in Nigel's car.

"Don't worry," he says. "Lucy was sympathetic. Guests come to Rocky Cove because they need to feel special. The minute they begin to think they're falling off the A-list, they put up some sort of stink. Last year Mrs. Winston complained that her waitress refused to remember how she liked her eggs prepared."

"And?"

Nigel smiles. "She refused to remember how Mrs. Winston liked her eggs prepared."

"So that's why she's not back."

Nigel takes a sip of his soda and smiles again. "Nah. It's not such a big deal. Trust me."

"Come on, you," Carly says, linking her arm with mine. "Dominic and Harrison are going to show us how to dig for mussels." Carly drags me down to the mudflats behind the house.

As instructed, I squat, place my hand under a rock in a tidal pool, and tear off a handful of clinging black shells, connected by a vine of seaweed. I carefully separate them and drop them into a pot Dominic has brought from the kitchen.

Barefoot, and seemingly bored already with this gathering, Carly skips from one rock to another as if on a balance beam.

"So where do you go to school?" Harrison asks her. Both boys remain close by, ready to catch her if she falls.

"Winsor," she replies, reaching out a hand to Dominic's shoulder.

I drop another batch of mussels into the pot and look over at Carly. *Is Winsor in Boston?* It's likely. I've heard of it before. Maybe Carly spends the school season in Boston and the summer with her father. Anyway, who cares? I'm just so happy she's here now.

Harrison reaches out and offers her a sip of his drink.

Carly looks over at me and smiles. "Look at how many mussels you've found, Nolie! You are queen of succulent shellfish!" She jumps off a rock, lifts the hem of her dress, and walks through the muck to where I'm digging. "So can we cook these now?"

"Right here on the beach," Harrison suggests.

"Wouldn't a gas range be easier?" asks Dominic.

"Sure," Harrison says. "But who wants to squeeze into that crowded kitchen? And besides, we'd have to share these with everyone."

"Good point!" Dominic says. "All we need is fresh water,

some matches—there's certainly enough wood around here—and some butter. Come on, Carly."

They go up to the kitchen for supplies, leaving Harrison and me to round up kindling and firewood.

"How are the swimming lessons?" I ask, trying to regulate my breathing.

"They're typically slow to start," Harrison says, breaking some dead branches off a tree. "First we have to give swim tests and then work with the program counselors to come up with schedules. I don't know why it has to be this way. It seems to me that the schedules could be planned before the campers arrive and we could just plug the kids in according to ability."

"You've suggested it? I mean—sorry, you probably have."

"Yeah, but you know how these places are with their long traditions. No one thinks to ask if the routines work. Everyone's hell-bent on doing things the way they've always been done."

Rocky Cove seems to operate the same way. For example, wouldn't it be easier if the waitresses had designated sections in one of the dining rooms where their tables were clustered together? That way we wouldn't have to spend so much time running from one room to the other, and guests could see exactly how hard their waitresses were working to please *everyone*.

I share my thoughts as we begin to build a little teepee fire structure, adding Nigel's insight. "Actually, they don't want you to treat them all the same—they want to feel unique, special."

"Like the summer," he says.

I look up, not understanding.

"Don't know how to explain this," he says, "but people who come to Maine want a summer that's . . . life-changing, transformational. I mean, if you go to Disney, you expect fun. And if you go to Vegas, you expect . . ." He fishes.

"Escape?" I offer.

"Right! I was going to say money, but it's more. It's escaping your own dull life for a while—usually by doing something incredibly foolish."

He bounces up from where he's squatting, combing his hair behind his ears, which for some reason makes my knees wobble. "But people who come to Maine want to . . . to live big," he says. "To be awestruck, to—"

Fall in love, I think, and feel myself blush.

"Embrace it," he says. "Make it theirs."

Yeah. Like I said.

"Supplies on the way!" Carly holds one handle of a pot

of splashing water. Dominic holds the other and, with his free hand, waves what must be butter and matches in the air. He's grinning from ear to ear.

Harrison watches Carly as she glides toward us and then looks at me as if to say, *See? She is the leap, the dive, the soar. She's summer.*

chapter 12

Okay, I may be inexperienced, but I've made it my goal to remember how all my guests like their eggs prepared. Mrs. Barnes? Poached on toast. The shoe girls (whose names are Justine and Maggie) like sunny-side down (Cheffie's specialty—he turns the stove off right after the flip). Mr. Winston likes scrambled, Mrs. Winston prefers soft-boiled with a runny yolk, and the four little ones never eat eggs. Never.

After the last of my guests leave, I quickly refill the salt and pepper shakers on my tables, make sure any stains are covered with fresh nappies, and race up to the barn. Just as the dining room procedures have not changed in the last one hundred years, neither has the waitresses' routine. We wake and serve breakfast until nine. Then we change into bathing suits and go down to the ocean docks to read, listen to tunes, gossip, and sleep (always sleep). It isn't the ocean beach I had imagined—in truth, the "beach" is a rocky shoreline leading to mudflats at low tide—but it is sea and sun. Around eleven thirty we head to the barn, throw on our uniforms, and serve lunch. After lunch it's back into bikinis, but we follow the sun to the lake beach. Here we read, listen to tunes, gossip, and try to ignore the little kids who do everything to get the attention of their waitresses, until dinnertime.

Lounging on the dock after breakfast, me with a copy of *Pride and Prejudice* on my lap—mandatory summer reading—Lucy explains that Nigel is a nephew of Pete's, and therefore, like all Lovells, he is expected to gain some understanding of the family business during his "imprint years."

"So that's why he never drinks or lets loose at the beach parties," I say.

Annie nods. "His older brother screwed up big-time when he was here. Nigel is expected to behave differently."

"He's being groomed," says Lucy.

Carly shoots me a "told you so" look.

Someone shouts and we all turn to look. It's Kevin coming down the hill.

"Hey, Cannolis," he calls.

"What are you shouting?" Brita asks.

"Cannolis. Carly, Nola—suppose I could call them

'Canola,' as in canola oil, but 'Cannolis' sounds so much nicer."

"And sweeter," I say.

"And yummy," Carly says.

"And *why* do you need the Cannolis?" Lucy asks.

"You had a phone call," he says, turning and walking back up to the inn.

"We *both* had a call?" I ask.

"I told Dom and Harrison to call us," Carly says, reaching for more sunscreen.

"You did?"

"Sure. I told Dominic you'd never had lobster before. He insisted on taking us to Eaton's, and I suggested that Harrison come too."

Brita looks at me. "You've never had lobster?" she asks.

"My mother is allergic to shellfish," I say. "Harrison agreed?"

"Of course he agreed. Why wouldn't he?"

Brita persists. "But why haven't *you* had lobster? You could have ordered one in a restaurant."

I know why, but I don't want to say, *Because my sister is sick, on a strictly vegan diet (one of the gazillion things she's been made to try), and when I'm with her, I won't eat things she can't eat.* Exactly why I needed this summer. I just shrug.

"Ack," Mariah says, throwing her *People* magazine down. "It's going to be one of those times."

"What do you mean?" Annie asks.

"Lucy has Will. Now Carly has Dominic and Nola has Harrison. Annie, you will no doubt be hooked up with Nigel before the summer's over."

Please let Mariah be psychic.

"What makes you say that?" Annie asks, but her pink cheeks give her hopes away.

"And me? I have leprous old Mr. Franklin at table eight."

"But you didn't mention me. I'm a single woman, Mariah," Brita says.

"Huh," Mariah snorts. "Not for long. You, Brita, are never single for long."

I don't even try to contradict Mariah. Maybe, like Annie, I harbor hope.

That night after work Harrison pulls up in front of the barn in an old Jeep, and I realize that without him, the vehicle-less Dominic wouldn't have transportation to Deer Isle—and to Eaton's Lobster Pool. Had Dominic asked to borrow the Jeep? Had Harrison suggested they double? Or had he kept things more open, saying, *Why don't the four of us go?* Maybe this was his way of staying in the Carly competition.

He comes around to open the passenger door, but Carly doesn't wait. Instead, she hoists herself up with the roll bar and into the backseat, laughing. Feeling like the maidenly aunt, I thank Harrison for opening my door as I climb in.

"So how is it, growing up outside of Boston and all, you haven't tried lobster?" Dominic asks me as we pass the live lobster tank on the way to our table.

"Well, I *have* tried eating those little legs," I say, taking a new tack this time. "My father brought home a lobster when I was little and gave me those spindly legs to suck on."

"Oh, the abused child," says Carly, "thrown mere morsels."

"You know, there was a law on the books during Colonial times," Harrison says, bringing his chair closer to the others, "that prohibited people from serving lobster to their servants more than twice a week."

"Poor peasants—some things haven't changed for the better," Dom says. He pulls a six-pack of beer from a cooler.

"You can do this?" I ask. "Drink your own beer in this restaurant?"

"Look around, Nolie," Carly says. "Everyone's brought their own."

"But we're—" I catch myself before shouting out that Carly and I are underage. "Sorry," I say.

The others look at one another and shake their heads. Naïve? Yes. Cute? Not. But they quickly forgive me and make a big deal of tying on my bib, demonstrating the use of the lobster crackers and the pick, and giving me little tips throughout the meal.

Carly makes a show of eating the tomalley (not for me, thank you). Harrison leans over to wipe some green stuff off her face with his finger, and I feel my heart snag. *Nothing you couldn't have guessed,* I tell myself. I mean, who wouldn't be attracted to Carly? *Let it go. Let* him *go.*

One pound of clams, one lobster, one baked potato, and two beers later, I'm feeling as if I may not be the world's most desired girl, but I have had the ideal meal. I look across the table and smile.

"Miss Nola, I do believe you're drunk," says Dominic.

"Drunk on this meal, maybe," I say, though I am feeling a wee bit tipsy. "I can't believe I've experienced seventeen years without lobster."

Harrison leans over and ruffles my hair. Dominic laughs.

Somehow I've become their pet. It's all right. It's still fun.

"I'm bored with this," says Carly. "What else can we do?"

chapter 13

"Pull over!" Carly shouts before we drive back onto the mainland.

Harrison takes a sharp left and parks in the lot of a dingy roadside motel.

"Let's go out on the bridge," she says.

"Not me," Harrison says, opening a tackle box between the front seats and pulling out a mega-pack of M&M's. "I'm happy right here."

I'm reminded of our first meeting when he told me he's a Taoist. Harrison has nothing to prove.

As he holds out the bag to me, I search my under-functioning brain for some reason to stay where I am. How about, *I'm wildly attracted to this guy, and maybe if you two leave, we'll jump each other* or . . . or . . . hell, I can't think of any other reason.

"Come on, you!" Carly says, pulling on my shoulder. I glance at Harrison, whose face poses a question.

An invitation? A test? I can't read it.

Carly stands by my side, waiting, and I slide out of the Jeep.

Dominic gives us a history lesson as we walk across the bridge in the fog. This is a suspension bridge spanning around 330 meters—supposedly the same design as the Tacoma Narrows Bridge in Washington, which collapsed like a ribbon in the wind.

I figure Dom's just trying to scare us.

But Carly's not scared. She walks to the center of the bridge and sits up on the railing. We move in closer to protect her.

"Hold my hands," she says.

We obey and she suddenly stands on the rail. Her hair and shirt blow in the breeze. She looks like some sort of goddess up there.

"What do you think you're doing, Carly?" Harrison calls, joining us after all.

"Do you believe in reincarnation?" Carly asks, seeming not to hear him.

"No," says Harrison. "When you're dead, you're dead. That's it."

I feel familiar fingers grabbing my heart and wish I'd called home . . . or written that promised letter. "I kind of believe in it," I say tentatively, reaching for the waistband of Carly's jeans with my free hand, "or at least life after death. But it might be wishful thinking."

"If I come back, I want to be a tree," says Carly, stretching her body upward. "A tall, majestic tree. I'd just stand, spreading my branches and growing taller every day—surrounded by all my tree friends."

"Come here, Miss Tree," says Harrison, holding his arms out.

Who could resist?

Carly jumps into that embrace, and the four of us lope arm in arm back to the Jeep.

"Are you all right?" Carly asks as we're getting into our pj's. "You've been quiet since the bridge."

I don't want her to think it's anything she's done—it isn't. "You know my little sister?"

"The one you write?"

I didn't know she'd noticed. "Yeah," I say. "She's really sick."

"Like . . . cancer?"

I nod.

Carly paces around the room. "But it's a good cancer, right? One of the curable kinds?"

I picture my mother's face as she says, "If one more person asks me if this tumor is the good kind, I'm going to scream. There is no good kind!" But Mom gets it, really, and so do I. People want to make things okay for us. You get used to it.

"She's doing chemo," I say, not sure if I'm trying to make myself or Carly feel better. "For the second time. But she's got a chance."

"Phew," says Carly. She comes over to where I'm sitting on the bed and gives me a big hug. "What's her name?"

"Song."

"Don't worry, Nola," she says, standing again. "She'll be fine. I like her name. Have I told you my doctor's name is Dr. Ache? And my dentist is Dr. Moss?"

She turns off the light and we lie in the dark. For a few moments I'm lost in my thoughts of Song, and then I'm not sure, but I think Carly might be crying.

"Are you okay?" I ask.

She sniffs. "My best friend in grade school died of cancer," she says. "Leukemia."

It's my turn to get up and hug her.

Chapter 14

It rains for the next week and we have no place to go.
The barn has been overtaken by cranky guests playing
cribbage or watching family movies that Nigel schedules
at regular intervals. The kids race around, pulling games
off the shelves and then abandoning them. Forget about
even getting near the computer—everyone is suddenly
desperate for outside contact.

At first we're all kind of psyched to hide out upstairs:
read, write postcards, learn something new (Annie taught
a few of us how to knit), but after days and days the barn
has become cold and damp and the rain on the roof is a
ceaseless drum.

Weather puts everything on pause: no beach parties, no
"spontaneous" meetings along the road, no chance of bump-
ing into someone during a run. Counselors at Robin Hood
are required to turn in all their electronics when they arrive
at camp—so texting with the guys isn't even an option.

"I can't stand another minute of hanging around here," Carly says, stretching out on her bed.

That's when we hear Nigel below. "I think that's a great idea, Mrs. Winston. I'm sure some of our staff would love to challenge the kids to a game of Monopoly."

Carly looks at me with fear in her eyes.

"Carly and Nola are upstairs, I think," says Annie. "I could get them."

"The Cannolis!" says Mrs. Winston. "The kids will be thrilled."

When did the guests start calling us that? Carly and I leap up and collide as we head out the door. I start to take the stairs, but she grabs my arm, "Too risky."

I follow her to Lucy and Brita's room; they are presumably holed up in the maintenance shack, watching a movie on Will's laptop. Carly shuts their door and then opens the window that faces a big maple tree at the back of the barn. It takes her three seconds to unfasten the screen, lift it out of place, and let it drop to the ground. "Hurry," she whispers.

There is no time to tell Carly that heights and I don't play well together, that I have never in my whole life climbed a tree—never mind a tree that's slimy from a week's worth of rain. I crouch on the windowsill and lean forward to grab the one branch that looks as if it might have a chance of holding me.

"You can do it, Nolie," she says, and I believe her. My foot slips when I try to step onto the tree, and I grasp at anything I can—sure that my arms are being pulled entirely from their sockets. Miraculously, I don't plummet to the ground. I regain some footing and freeze for a few moments, letting my heart slow down.

We can hear Annie calling us, and with that, we climb downward, finally shimmying to the ground. My belly is badly scratched, we're covered in mud and bark, but we're laughing.

Carly takes my hand as we make our way through the woods, and I wonder why people stay inside when it rains. The woods are magical when wet. Colors I probably wouldn't even notice—lime green moss, red mushrooms, and yellow wildflowers—glow in the drenched half-light.

"Watch," says Carly, turning over a big rock. Some bugs scramble away, but just sitting there is an orange spotted newt.

"He's so cute!" I say. "How could you have possibly known he'd be there?"

She shrugs, like she made him happen.

The woods end abruptly, and we find ourselves standing

on the edge of a rock cliff. Both the small patch of grass at the top and the layered rock are slippery, and I instinctually grab on to an evergreen shrub to ensure that I stay right where I am. To our right are scrubby paths that probably follow a gradual descent to the ocean docks. The waves below are churning and crashing from all the rain.

"This must be the ledges," I say.

"What ledges?"

I tell her about the Rocky Cove tradition and try to imagine leaping.

She's suddenly afire. "Let's do it now," she says. "Let's be the first to jump from them this summer."

"No way," I tell her, lifting my shirt to show her my bloody torso. "I've had enough injury for one day."

She raises her face to the sky, letting the rain hit her skin directly. "Okay. But we are so doing this."

I raise my eyebrows in question.

"*Nola,*" she chants.

"All right," I whisper.

"Now you're sizzling."

chapter 15

The sun finally makes its reappearance. I'm rocking on the porch after lunch, waiting for the other waitresses to finish up. I have a letter from Song, a single haiku:

> *Don't write just bad stuff*
> *You don't have to hide good things*
> *Write: Wish you were here*

It's pretty good, I think. Not all of Song's haikus are. She often writes stuff she knows nothing about, like passionate, undying love. Those haikus come across as, I don't know, silly. Thin teenish.

But this one? This one hits the mark. I feel a wash of guilt. Maybe I have been keeping the fun from Song, fearing she'll feel left out. Maybe I'm feeling guilty about having a life separate from her.

Nigel drops down beside me.

He has a pile of college catalogs in his lap. "Where you applying?" he asks.

"No clue," I say. I know that I should have some idea by now. But college is expensive. And it's hard for me to think about being away from Song for any longer than I already will be this summer. If she's still sick, I'm not going anywhere. "How about you?"

"Not a question of where I *want* to go. It's a given. Colgate. My great-grandfather went to Colgate, as did his son and *his* son before me."

"You didn't tell, did you?" Lucy asks, slamming the screen door behind her.

"Nope," Nigel says. "Not a word."

"Tell what?" asks Carly, who follows behind Lucy. She plops down on my knee.

I don't mind. I wait to hear what hasn't been told, but apparently, Nigel and Lucy aren't ready to spill.

They chat about the revised time-off schedule—everyone on staff gets one day a week (mine's Friday)—until all of us are congregated on the porch.

"Come on," says Nigel. "Let's move to the barn."

"A meeting?" I ask.

"You were out running when I announced it," says Lucy.

Carly shrugs, meaning, *I guess we'll find out.*

Once we're comfortable in the rec room, Lucy says

that she and Nigel have worked out a plan for this year's staff show.

Nigel says with authority, "We've decided not to do a talent show."

"What?" the crowd roars.

"We're doing a play," Lucy says.

Nigel gives us a chance to process this (most think it's a good idea since they've performed their funniest talents in past years) and then tells us, "We're doing the murder mystery *And Then There Were None.*"

"Oh my God!" says Mariah. "My cousin was in that play last year. It's terrifying!" And then she quickly adds, "I'll play the butler's wife. She's sooo fraaagile." She gives us her performance of an old woman fainting.

"You look like the typical Rocky Cove guest," Annie says.

"The part's yours," says Lucy.

"Lucy's our casting director," says Nigel.

Lucy looks around. "But if anyone else wants the job . . ."

No one says a word.

"Okay then," Lucy says. "I thought we could take turns tomorrow reading Vera's and Phil's parts—I guess you'd call them the leads—and then I'll just go ahead and assign the other roles." Nigel passes out scripts from a stack he produces, and we fool around with lines for a few minutes.

I'm psyched. Song and I perform for each other or my parents all the time, but I've never been in a real play. I've always run, and clocking the necessary mileage hasn't left time for much else—not if I was going to be a contender.

None of the other waitresses seem to think about the audition for the rest of the day. But the idea of performing in front of people—even if it's just the waitresses and the maintenance guys—flips me into training mode. So I sneak off with the script hidden in my shorts to practice.

In the character notes Vera is described as intelligent and capable but prone to hysteria. (This is a part Song would *love* to perform.) I recite some of her lines, sounding ridiculous at first, but eventually, I begin to feel it. I feel the melodramatic Vera. My confidence starts to grow.

Acting is a lot like running. If you're on, both allow you to escape the confines of your body, of your life.

I feel the typical nerves (hello, Fear and Doubt) as we gather to audition. But I give myself my usual pep talk— telling myself I'm prepared. And besides, this is a summer staff production, for criminy's sake; most of us have probably had little time on a stage.

Wrong. Brita is unbelievable. She becomes another

person before our eyes. Her Vera is commanding and larger than life.

Carly reads next. She's good too! It's as if she's duplicating Brita but tweaking her performance in just the right places. I'm amazed. And so out of my league.

By the time my turn comes around, it's clear I'll probably be playing one of the men in the cast—the one who chokes in the first ten minutes. I start reading Vera's lines, but I feel way too much like myself. It makes me mad (I didn't sound like this when I was practicing), so I make a point to pump up the stage directions. *Vera: jumpy and highly reactive.*

And then something happens. It's as if I—or, rather, the girl I'm playing—is sick and tired of being simply capable and so transforms into something else. My words are intelligent, but I can hear my voice becoming shriller— more high-strung. My hands flutter around; my body moves in ways that begin to feel totally foreign.

Everyone is laughing— I *am* making a total fool of myself—but I keep going. I've never had center stage before, and at any moment I will have to give it up. Acting over the top is scary, I admit. Really scary. But fun, too. I read far beyond the designated lines.

When I finally stop, Lucy has tears running down her

face. "You've got it, girl," she says. "You have *got* to play Vera."

And then as an afterthought she turns to Brita and mouths, *Is that okay with you?* in a totally understanding and supportive way.

Brita nods back. "I'll be Inspector Blore," she says.

If it were possible, my whole body would be smiling. I look at Carly, knowing she's going to tell me I'm sizzling, but she's turned away.

"What part would you like, Carly?" Lucy asks.

She shrugs in a nonchalant way. "I'll be the understudy." Then she gets up and goes through the back door to our rooms.

Later she barely acknowledges my hello.

"What's going on?" I ask. "Did I say or do something wrong?"

"I don't know, did you?"

How am I supposed to answer this? I'm not usually this clueless. My mind sorts, frantically. The last thing in the world I want is to ruin anything between us. Is Carly pissed because I got the lead? Should I have asked if she wanted to play Vera, the way Lucy had checked things out with Brita?

"I just get tired of Lucy and Nigel running things around here."

I can't help thinking it's more complicated than that. "Well, it's only us now. What do you want to do?" I mean, *What part do you want in the play?* But Carly hears me differently.

Her face brightens. "You're right. Let's skip the beach this afternoon. Let's do something . . . just the two of us. See if we can find Dom and Harrison."

"How?" I ask, hoping to sound open-minded. "They're working. They can't spend time with us."

"I know!" Carly says. "Let's take the rowboat out on the pond! Harrison will definitely be down on the docks, and who knows, if we get really lucky, Dom's group will be there too."

The rowboat sounds fun. And different. But wouldn't we look desperate?

"Don't worry," says Carly, reading my mind. "We'll keep our backs turned to shore. We won't turn around and wave or anything until they're on a megaphone to get our attention."

"And what'll we be doing?"

Carly's eyes grow wide with a new idea. "Fishing!"

"Fishing?"

"Not us. Stella!"

"Stella's coming too?"

"Of course. Stella will love it. Her babysitter—what's her name? She will love us for taking Stella off her hands."

"Camp counselors!" I say, getting into it, shutting out the piece of my brain that whispers, *How did we get to* here?

Chapter 16

Right after lunch we're sitting in the middle of Horseshoe Pond. I pull up the oars and attempt to untangle the line on Stella's small fishing rod.

"But, Nola," she says, "I need something to go on my hook. We forgot to dig up any worms."

"Hmm, that *is* a problem," says Carly, leaning over her shoulder. "You don't have one of those fancy flies in your tackle box?"

Stella looks as if a fishing lure might suddenly appear. "Uh-uh," she says.

"Well, drop your line and maybe the fish will bite anyway," Carly says.

"Why?" asks Stella.

"Why what, Stella Bella?"

"Why would the fish bite anyway?"

Carly looks at me as if to say, *You try.*

"I have an idea," I say. "Fish like wiggly things, right?"

"Like worms," says Stella, nodding.

"And sparkly things?"

She thinks for a moment. "Like other little fish."

"Then how about this?" I reach down and gently tug the hair elastic with its sparkly bobble out of Stella's hair.

She pushes her hair away from her forehead and watches me tie the band around the hook.

"What do you think, Stella?" I ask.

Her whole face lifts. "Watch out!" she shouts, and tosses the line into the water.

The sun is shining through the tiniest wisps of clouds, glinting on the pond. Quietly, I take one oar and slip it onto the water to keep the boat from drifting too close to the Robin Hood shore.

"Don't look now," whispers Carly, but of course Stella looks right away.

"Harrison!" she yells. "Harrison, I'm fishing!"

Harrison is crouched on the edge of the dock, giving instructions to a group of shivering boys. Then he blows his whistle and directs them up to the bleachers to get their towels. When the last boy has left the waterfront, Harrison walks to the end of the docks and yells to Stella.

"Caught anything?"

"Not yet. I'm feeding them hair bands!"

"Hair bands? What kind of bait is that?"

"Come see for yourself," Carly calls.

I jump as the oar slips from the lock and crashes down on the seats.

"Such grace," says Carly.

Harrison loosens a kayak from the end of the dock, crouches into it, and paddles out to us. No tap of paddle against fiberglass, no splashes of water in the air. He's a reflection shimmering on the surface.

"See?" Stella says, reeling her line in to show off her bait.

"And what will you catch with that?" he asks, resting his paddle across the kayak and looking directly at me.

My flapping fish of a heart tries to leap from the boat.

"Lox," I try.

He flicks me a wide smile.

"We're geniuses, don't you think?" says Carly, resting her hands on my seat and leaning closer to him. Her long hair fans against my bare shoulder. "We didn't have bait so we improvised."

The kayak rocks, sending ripples in all directions. "Only you, Miss Tree," he says slowly, as if not sure what his reaction should be, "could think of something *so* creative."

"I'll take that as a compliment," she says. "The best compliment."

"Even though the hair band was my idea?" I ask. I'm teasing, but maybe only half teasing.

"What do you mean?" Carly asks.

"Stella probably won't catch anything, but the thing was *my* invention."

"If you say so, Nola," Carly says in the way you might pacify a child who insists she's not tired. She shoots Harrison a look that implies I'm being a tad neurotic.

"How about *you* say so?"

Carly stares at me, first with disbelief and then with obvious annoyance. "You want me to say, Nola, that using a hair band was your idea?"

"Yes," I say. *Wow. Where did that come from?*

"And then you will stop being so ridiculously competitive?"

"I don't want to fish anymore," says Stella, wrapping herself around my arm.

"Neither do I," says Carly. She turns to Harrison and adds, "Maybe I'll see you later." Not maybe *we'll* see you later.

Carly grabs at the oars. I move to the front seat in the boat and brace myself for what's to come.

She rows with a vengeance. As we're pulling the boat up onto the sand, she says in a pained, but nevertheless angry voice, "I can't believe you attacked me out there. I would never have humiliated you in that way. Believe it or not, Nola, *I* care about you."

"I wasn't attacking you," I say. But I'm confused. Was I defending myself? Or *was* I attacking?

Carly turns and heads up the hill without me.

I reach for Stella's hand.

"It was *your* idea," she whispers.

Chapter 17

"Nola!" Kevin is standing in the doorway to the kitchen with his white apron tied around his waist. "Tomorrow's your day off, yes?"

"It is," I say, walking over to him. I haven't given it much thought. Without a car, there's little to mark a day off.

"Mine too. Want to see Isle au Haut?"

"An island? Like Deer Isle?"

"No, much tinier, only a few houses. But there's hiking trails that wind around the cliffs—you could run if you wanted—and these beaches covered in stones. You know the kind rubbed down by the ocean? Stones the size of ostrich eggs."

Kevin, hiking? I wouldn't have guessed. Is he asking me out? But no—there's no nervousness, no flirting, no electricity. Everything about him says he's just drumming up a friend.

"And on the way back," he continues, "I thought we

could eat at Fire Pond—my treat. The chef there's from France, and there's this dish . . ."

It sounds fun and I tell him so. Slowly, I'm becoming part of this place, I think, patting the script in my pocket. Each day belonging a little more. I practically skip to the barn.

And am totally shocked to see Harrison standing at the door.

"Hey," he says.

"Hey, yourself," I say, which I think sounds quite cool considering I am about to wet my pants. I'm glad I didn't *really* skip. "Where're you headed?"

"Here. Wanted to see if you had any interest in the square dance tonight."

"Definitely!" I say. "I mean, I've never done it and I'll probably make a total ass of myself but—"

He glances up at the windows on the second floor. "That's where you live, right?"

"Right."

"Oh, and Carly's invited too," he says.

My formerly speeding heart hits a wall. So I'm not the one Harrison was hoping to bump into. "I'll tell her."

"Okay then," he says, smiling, and then waves as he heads back to camp.

I go up to my room and grab my notebook—mostly to distract myself from obsessing over Harrison and what he might be thinking—and finally write to Song.

But . . . I let myself know the truth . . . I've been avoiding writing for days. It's not that I don't think about Song—I do, all the time. *Will the world end if I actually own my own summer, have my life to myself for one short month or two, though?* The thought shocks me. I pick up the pen and write:

Song, my Song,

This is my favorite day of the week at Rocky Cove. Instead of serving in the dining room, we have a lobster picnic on the beach. And we don't have to wear our dreaded uniforms! We can wear short-sleeved shirts and jeans since we spend most of our time carrying platters of steaming lobsters from a big boiler to guests hanging out on the rocks.

Some of them pretend to be incapable "flatlanders" and ask their waitresses to shell their lobsters. Most attempt to have the true Maine experience, but they eventually give up on the messy process and leave claws or even the tails sitting on their plates. The moment the last guest has made his or her way up the hill, we jump in and feast on the remains. I know this probably sounds disgusting to someone who's a vegan, but when you get better, Song, I'm treating you to your first.

Gotta go. It's off to the square dance at the Bucks Harbor Yacht Club. A counselor from the boys' camp, Harrison, asked me. I know, stop laughing. Me, square dancing, does make a pretty insane picture.

Oh, and there's more! Did I tell you that we're putting on a play? Guess who got the lead? Me!

Lots of love,

Nola

    Cracking crustaceans
    Difficult. But watch this girl
    Come out of her shell

chapter 18

As we walk into the yacht club, Harrison, pretending to be a host on some nature show, gives us the distinguishing features and habitat of the crowd: Club members can be sighted at the doors greeting people and generally looking like they own the place; tourists arriving on schooners are frequently found gathered on the porch in navy blazers and sundresses, talking loudly about their boats; Rocky Cove and Robin Hood staff cling to the back walls as if in junior high; and die-hard square dancers (women in petticoats, men in country-style shirts with lanyards) do-si-do across the floor.

And I discover, to my surprise, that Pete and Susanna are serious square dancers.

Harrison and Dominic hang by me and Carly—or should I say, more honestly, both boys circle around her. Although Carly and I often mention the two guys' names, usually when we're joking around, we have never actually shared our feelings about them. Which one does Carly want? Dominic? I'd originally assumed so, since they'd had so much fun together when we cooked mussels and she took him up on his invitation for a lobster dinner. On the other hand, it was Carly who made sure Harrison went too. I thought she was doing me a favor—wanted me along on the excursion—but what if she's more interested in Harrison? *Shut up, Nola. Some friend you are.* But still . . .

Once, for about five minutes, my cousin Georgia and I liked the same guy. Neither of us said a word to the other. If we had, we'd have had to admit we were competing. One of us would have felt compelled to fold. So we let the guy pick. Didn't pick either of us! Maybe Carly and I are playing the same game.

At that moment she reaches out and takes my hand. "Come on, Nolie. If these two guys aren't going to ask us to dance, we'll dance together."

Harrison doesn't miss a beat. He takes Dominic's elbow and leads him out on the floor. Dom plays the bashful female as we create our square. As it turns out, none of us has a clue when it comes to square dancing, but at the yacht club no one really cares—not even the diehards who smile in that "remember the first time we tried?" way.

We're out on the porch waiting for the guys to bring us punch (how scrapbookish) when I tell Carly about Kevin's invitation.

"You can't go!"

"Why not?"

"Lucy offered to cover for me tomorrow since most of my tables asked for picnic lunches. And I'm borrowing Mariah's car—I want to show you Castine."

"What?"

"It's a fishing village. You'll love it, Nola."

"But why didn't you tell me?"

"I wanted to surprise you."

Nice gesture, but what about Kevin? As usual, Carly knows what I'm thinking.

"Tell him you changed your mind." She makes it sound so simple. But it feels bad.

No, wait. I have a thought. "Why don't we ask Kevin to come with us. To Castine?" I'm hoping there's a restaurant equal to the Fire Pond there.

Carly pouts. "I want it to be just the *two* of us," she says.

Suddenly, I feel owned. Why can't she just step back for one moment and ask what *I* want?

Carly slips her arm through mine. "Don't you think,

Nola, you might be inflating your importance when it comes to Kevin? I'm sure he asked you out of kindness—you're the new girl, you have the same day off, and you've never seen Isle au Haut or gone to the Fire Pond. It was nice. But he's not going to care if you change your plans."

Now I feel ridiculous.

"*He* docs have other friends, you know."

Dominic suggests we leave the dance to climb Lookout Hill. Why not? Something significant might happen—something that will change the order of things—and I suddenly, desperately want to know what the new order will be.

We don't have a flashlight, but navigating our way by moonlight isn't hard. Carly, who drank from a flask offered by a hopeful but unlucky sailor, seems less sure-footed and keeps reaching out for one of the guys. "Where are you leading us?" she asks.

"Come with me," Dominic says. He wraps his arm around her waist and leads her to the top of the hill.

Did the guys plan this? The spray of stars across the sky and the dancing lights from boats below make the night seem surreal.

"Come see," Dominic says to Carly, pulling her back down another path.

"There's a sort of cave down there," Harrison says, parking himself on a rock. "Guys call it 'the grotto.'"

I sit next to him.

"Do you run cross-country for school?" he asks, recalling our first meeting up here.

"Yup."

"Three-mile races?"

"Three point one."

"Your best time?"

"Eighteen."

I can see him calculating in his head. "No way!"

I smile.

"You're kiddin' me. That's, like, a five point—"

"Five point eight." I love people being surprised. I guess I don't look (dress? act?) like the typical athlete.

"How long you been running?"

"Five years."

"In the big races?"

"Some. But mostly I run for school. It's not like I have a private coach or anything. How about you? Do you have a sport?"

"Swim team."

"Oh, sorry. I should have known that," I say.

"What are you apologizing for—you've never seen

me swim. You know, you apologize a lot."

"I do?" I'm not sure if I should take this as criticism or a sign that Harrison is interested enough to pay attention. I start shivering.

He pulls his sweatshirt over his head and hands it to me. "Here."

I shake my head—he needs it as much as I do—but he puts it on me like I'm a little kid.

"That's enough, you two," says Carly, coming back up the path. Dominic looks as confused as I feel.

"Did you guys know that Nola is a star athlete?" asks Harrison.

"Oh yeah?" Dominic asks.

Carly drops down on the other side of Harrison. "She runs fast. She's got reason to. She's angry."

Whoa!

Harrison looks at me.

I don't say a thing.

"Her sister has a brain tumor. That's how she deals."

"Really?" Harrison whispers.

The rock beneath me turns sharp and cold. My chest feels exactly the way it did when my parents told me that Song's tumor had returned. A life term extended.

Carly just changed everything. Will Harrison share his

own concerns, his personal fears, *his* worries with me now? Of course not. Everything seems trivial in light of a sister with cancer. There's a sting in the back of my throat.

He studies the jagged hem of his jeans. Any heat that might have been building has floated off into the ether.

You would think that I'd have some remark—an optimistic quote, a funny retort—to ease the situation. You know, hit the ball over the net and then jump the net to hit it back to myself . . . that sort of thing. But I've never come up with more than a quick "Such is life," and I use it now.

And after a mumbled "Shit" and an "Oh, that's tough," we make our way back down the hill.

"Why are you so pissy?" Carly asks when we get back to the barn.

"Shhh. Some people are sleeping."

"Who cares? They've kept us awake plenty of times."

I whip off my clothes. "Why did you tell the guys about Song?"

"Ugh," she says, rolling back on her bed. "You didn't tell me not to."

"Didn't think I had to. That information's *mine*." I exhale for what seems like the first time since she opened her mouth.

Carly sits up and, holding the bed frame with both hands, leans forward. "I thought we were friends, Nola. I thought you trusted me. I wouldn't do *anything* to hurt you. I don't imagine an invisible line down the middle of this room: This is Nola's, this is mine. And I definitely don't imagine an invisible line down the middle of our lives."

"I'm sorry," I say, sitting on my bed across from her. "It's just that —isn't it possible that I might just be good at running?"

"Of course you are," she says, coming over to give me a hug. "Consider my saying anything a favor," she says. "You have no idea how Harrison feels about you. If he was planning a quick hook-up, he'd think twice now, wouldn't he? I didn't want him messing around with you, Nolie. I guess I feel protective."

We get into bed and I let the knots unravel. What Carly said may make sense. But what helps the most is that she picked up on my interest in Harrison. What felt like a betrayal a minute ago now feels a little like a gift.

I pull out my phone and text Kevin, letting him know I won't be able to make it to the island after all.

Chapter 19

Castine, Maine, is like a postcard. We drive around for a few minutes so Carly can point out a few of the landmarks, and then we get out and walk. We wander down to the harbor and sit in the sun for a while. We're both quiet. I hope Kevin got my text (so far no answer) and replay the best bits with Harrison from the night before. It feels all too familiar until it occurs to me that we don't have to race up to the barn and throw on our uniforms for the next meal. Sweet.

When I announce that I'm hungry, Carly says she knows just the place. That's when I realize I really don't know that much about Carly's life—like how does she know Castine so well? How much time does she spend with each parent, and which one lives in Maine?

"Come on." Carly leads me into a bookstore called the Compass Rose. We pass books and toys and gifts on the way to the café, and I notice the cutest baby bib. My chest tightens. It reminds me of Bridget. Like, I still feel I did something wrong, but . . .

"What?" asks Carly.

For some reason—avoidance of the subject, I guess—I move my fingers over to a little silver frog. "I want this," I tell Carly.

"A frog?"

"I don't know why," I say.

"It's those long legs," she says.

We both order tomato bisque and crab quiche, and I ask Carly about her family.

"My mother lives in Boston," she says, "and so does my younger sister."

"You have a younger sister too?" I feel selfish about not asking until now.

"Wendy," she offers, "and we *don't* get along. She's crazy, Nolie. She has this wild temper and will go after me— physically—for the littlest of things. So I basically spend most of my time with my dad."

"Does that bother you?"

"No, my dad's pretty cool. And this way I get to keep my eyeballs in their sockets. I wouldn't be a bit surprised if there's something seriously wrong with Wendy."

"God, that sounds really hard."

"Well, yeah," says Carly. "But having a friend like you makes up for it."

I smile, thinking about the ways in which our lives are alike.

We finish our lunch and browse the books. It turns out that Carly and I have another thing in common: We were both huge fans of the Little Sister books when we were young—we can even recite the part about Karen having two of everything. I go in search of a book to buy, one to read when I've finished *Pride and Prejudice* (I may even choose another Jane Austen), but Carly keeps interrupting me to show me a book that she loved, loved, loved, and in the end I get nothing.

The day seems implausibly bright as we finally leave the store. While Carly hops into a shop to price some sandals she saw in the window, I check my phone. I finally have a message from Kevin:

```
ok, hiked, swam, ate homemade
rhubarb pie at fabulous
roadside stand. can finally
forgive. your loss
```

I don't know Kevin well enough to know if he's kidding. I start to read it to Carly . . . and then decide not to.

As we're driving back to Rocky Cove, she suddenly pulls into the parking lot of Hair Extraordinaire. "I'm tired of this bale of straw," she says, pulling on her long hair. "Let's go see if they take walk-ins."

Sure enough, they do. I sit and watch Carly get her hair cut, my thoughts turning first puzzled and then as confused and dark as they've ever been.

Later wanting to avoid everyone in the barn, I write to Song:

Song, Song, Blue—

I just tried to call you, but your phone is off, and I don't want to talk to Mom at the moment. I really wish you and I were sitting in the hammock right now and I was telling you about my day, and you were able to say all the right things that make me feel like I'm a stupid fool, but nevertheless better.

Carly and I visited a little coastal town for the day and had a GREAT time. On the way home, we stopped so she could get a haircut. You know how sick I was of my long hair, so I totally got this.

While she had her hair cut, I sat in the corner reading *People*. (Reminded me of you. How many of those do you think we've read in doctors' offices, anyway?) I could hear Carly saying things like, "Can you cut it shorter here? How about making this part a little spunkier?" I was getting more curious by the moment.

But here's the thing. Carly got the same cut as mine. Not close . . . exactly the same! She even had red added to her bangs. Is that weird? It felt weird. She thought I would love it, but I don't. (Song, this is where you can tell me I'm an ass.)

Of course, Carly being Carly (she misses nothing) knew I wasn't thrilled. "You really don't think you discovered impish, do you?" she said, and then pointed out that the hairdresser in Castine suggested the very same cut as a hairdresser in Walpole, Massachusetts. "Something tells me there are others out there looking like us," she said.

Are my feelings absurd? I admit that Carly has a point. It's not as if I designed the cut. And what's the quest to look different about, anyway? Annie and I have the same jeans. Lucy and I have the same Gap sweatshirt. This doesn't bother me. So why am I exasperated by the haircut?

And now as I write this letter, I think of you, Song, and the fact that you've lost all of your hair and I can't believe I'm being so utterly self-centered and ridiculous. (God, I'm crying.) See? We don't even have to be in the same state and you set me straight.

Your jerk sister who loves you,

Nola

Glistening blue eyes
Laughter flows over boulders
Song is not her hair

"Give me a piece of your notebook paper," Carly says.

I didn't realize she'd come into the room. I do a double take every time I see her. Her hair makes her look *that* different. I tear out a page, wondering if she can tell I've been crying.

"Dear Song," she says as she writes.

I sit right up, expecting her to write something mean, something sarcastic: *Dear Song. Your sister is having a bird over my new haircut.*

Instead, she reads: "I'm your sister's friend Carly. She has told me so much about you—what a cool kid you are and how brave you've been. She's also told me that you love to draw. I'm looking forward to seeing your art one day."

"What are you doing?" I ask.

"I thought Song might appreciate getting more mail. It's got to be incredibly boring sitting around in hospitals."

She continues: "Your sister, Nolie, is a pretty great kid too. Except when she makes that face like the one she's making right now. I bet you know it, Song. It's that face that says, 'Are you picking on me?' But we wouldn't do that to Nola, would we?"

Carly goes on to tell Song all kinds of details about our lives up here—things I haven't thought to tell her. Like how there's supposedly a ghost in one of the cabins and how one of the guests used to be in a famous band. Then she begs an envelope, writes my home address (how the hell does she know my address?), and asks for a stamp.

As I walk down to the office with both envelopes, I

imagine Song reading these letters. She'll smile at Carly's description of each staff member, especially Cheffie. Wish I could say the thought makes me happy.

It occurs to me that I don't have to send Carly's letter. I could pocket it—no one would be the wiser.

But then I remember the contents of my letter. I swing open the office door, drop Carly's letter into the out-box, and guide mine through the office shredder.

Chapter 20

I cannot sort out my Carly feelings, and I'm so tired of trying after a while that I practically sprint to acting practice, where I can focus on what I'm learning and forget everything else. I like acting a lot. Especially rehearsing. The others are helpful and supportive, and I'm beginning to feel I might be good at this. I've felt accomplished before. I do fairly well in school and I usually place in cross-country and track races. But this feels different somehow. There is a more collective feeling of success. It's a rush to see Lucy and Nigel so excited. And the excitement is catchy. The better each of us gets, the better all of us get. The guests are already telling us that they're looking forward to the performance.

There is this one scene when Kevin touches my shoulder and I'm supposed to jump a mile. Even though we've practiced this moment a hundred times, I'm still genuinely startled when he does it.

"Nola, you make me laugh every time," Brita says. "You are so friggin' real in that scene!"

"A natural," says Annie.

Carly, sitting on the sidelines ready to cue our lines if we forget them, pipes up. "Nolie loves to be the center of attention."

I don't laugh. I don't contradict her. I pretend not to hear. But the words go to that deep place where barbs stick permanently. They grow into a tangled, thorny bush in which one vine is no longer distinguishable from the others.

I avoid talking to anyone after rehearsal. Instead, I run upstairs and dig through my growing pile of dirty clothes for something to run in. I grab my trainers and, damn it, the left lace breaks off in my hand. I fashion a crude knot, pull the laces as tight as I possibly can, and take off.

Center of attention. Center of attention. My feet pound out the beat.

I remember a time soon after Song had a relapse. I'd been fretting about not making high honors my fourth quarter of sophomore year. But my last quiz in American history must have bumped me up; I'd received an A after all. As I danced around the kitchen, my mother stared at me with a totally blank look on her face. How could I celebrate something as stupid as a grade? How could I be acting so big when my sister's life hung in the balance?

Carly is wrong, I think as I sprint up the hill before me. The center of attention is a target. A place for others to direct all of their anger or worries. Or, in Carly's case, jealousy. No, let someone else be the center of attention.

I run, and run, and run—run until all my anger, my fuel is depleted.

Then, as I jog my way back to Rocky Cove, I wonder.

Could Carly be right? Do I like attention? (*Doesn't everyone? Well, maybe not the truly shy.*) But didn't I come to Maine so I could be, just for a brief time, the center of my own life? Is that a terrible thing to admit? *Maybe.*

Maybe yes. Because if I'm *really* honest, rock-bottom honest, I'm sick of every single minute of every single day being about Song.

My eyes well up with tears. But there, I've said it. Might as well be honest.

I'm surprised, I think, as I walk down to the barn, that Carly doesn't know this hateful thing about me.

Or . . . maybe she does.

Chapter 21

I find myself looking for ways to put a little space between Carly and me, which is confusing. I mean, she has been my road into this amazing world—and without her, Harrison may not have given me the time of day. But I can't help it. I feel alternately disloyal, stupid, and . . . well . . . stubborn.

So, instead of going down to the ocean docks after breakfast, I head to the lake. The sun won't be on the beach, but it will be nice for swimming, and anyway, I should be doing more cross training for the fall.

When I get down there, I'm surprised to find I'm not alone. Annie is standing on the shoreline. She turns pink as Nigel pops out of the hut in his swimsuit. Huh. I've never seen Nigel swim.

"His day off," Annie is quick to tell me.

I realize the two of them had probably counted on the beach being empty first thing in the morning, and I try to figure out a way to excuse myself.

"It's a half mile across the lake," Nigel says. "Swim it with us."

"You guys don't—"

"No, really," says Annie. "It'll be fun."

"By the time we get back," Nigel adds, "there will be families on this beach. It will look better if Annie and I have a chaperone." He smiles.

As I swim beside these two, I think about Nigel. Does he embody all things Rocky Cove, or is he afraid of the consequences of breaking out? (What are the consequences?) Does he mind the choices he has to make?

The swim is exactly what I need. But it isn't long before my freestyle breaks down and I do a steady breaststroke to the opposite shore, every now and then doing the backstroke to give my knees a break. We reach shallow water together and scramble up on a patch of sunny sand.

On our backs, musing about random things (like how I'm going to get the sand out of my hair in time for lunch), I come right out and ask Nigel what it means to be Pete's nephew. "What would happen if you got caught doing something—say, drinking?"

I expect him to say that Pete would send him packing like his brother or that his parents wouldn't forgive him.

He sighs. "Everything is mapped out for me: where I'll go to school, what I'll do when I graduate, how much money I'll make. I'm saving my energy—and their disappointment—for the bigger battles."

"Yeah, sure," says Annie. "You're just a wimp."

"A wimp?" Nigel sits up to see if Annie's kidding. "A wimp?"

She's smiling, but in a challenging way.

He extends his foot to push her on the shoulder.

She gets up to thump him on the head, and then there is yelping and tumbling . . . resulting in Annie sitting on Nigel's lap.

Forgotten, I get up and stroll into the water. The thought of warm arms and legs entangled, and noses nuzzling into salty necks, makes my whole body ache.

Thankfully, it's not long before they join me again, and the three of us, with a good strong pace, make our way back.

"Looks like someone is waiting for us," says Annie when the Rocky Cove beach is in clear sight.

It's Carly, wearing my favorite shirt.

"I had no idea where you were!" she cries. "I thought you might have gone for a run, but your sneakers were still in the room."

Before I can respond, Nigel does: "I *have* seen you before, Carly Whitehouse. I remember now. You were at the American Legion dance last summer. You danced with—"

"Don't even get me started on your brother," says Carly, laughing, forgetting all about my abandonment.

Chapter 22

And Then There Were None is about ten people trapped on an island with no chance of escaping one another's company—and I'm beginning to feel as if it's mirroring my reality. I like the people I'm trapped with (though I am getting increasingly tired of one), but I sense summer is on the downslope.

I decide to run in search of Harrison, and I head to Lookout Hill, hoping Providence will have a hand in our meeting like it did the first time.

No such luck. There's no sign of life here on this hill. Okay, so the possibility was extremely remote, and I'm just playing with wishful thinking, but I can't help myself. It's late afternoon. If Harrison is not down at the waterfront, he's probably kicking back in his cabin or maybe hanging out at . . . what did he call it? Hostess House?

I run down to the lake.

Fortunately, the others aren't there and neither are any

guests. I walk to the edge of the water, as if I'm here just for a cooldown stretch, and look over to the Robin Hood docks. Boys of all ages are leaping off them. Must be free swim. I don't see Harrison, but Josh, another waterfront counselor, recognizes me and waves. I wave back, turn, and run up the hill.

So where is this Hostess House? I wonder. On the edge of camp, Harrison said. Does that mean in the woods or along the road? There's a path on my left before the main road, and I decide to follow it. This is a foolish hunt, but I don't care.

Up ahead there's a cabin, and I can hear laughter inside. A counselor, someone I recognize from the square dance, starts out the front door, and suddenly, I don't know what to do. The path dead-ends. Do I pretend I'm lost? Turn around and run back?

He says over his shoulder, "Harrison, I think there's someone here for you."

Clearly, I haven't been as subtle as I thought.

My heart is pounding—and it's not from the run. Now that I've obviously sought him out, what do I say?

"Where's your counterpart?" Harrison asks from the door.

"I was running," I say, as if that explains everything.

"How many miles?"

I laugh. "Not many."

Awkward silence. We both dive in with a new question, but I'm happy to yield to his.

"How much time do you have before dinner?" he asks.

I look at my watch. "Twenty minutes." (If I cut out dinner for myself, I can go straight to waitressing.) "No, forty."

"Come with me."

He takes my hand and leads me through the woods, and I feel simultaneously calm and exhilarated. Calm because he seems to know me in a way that requires no explanation. I came looking for him. End of story. Exhilarated . . . well, because I am.

We arrive at a cabin that's a reasonable distance from the others. The camp laundry. It has that warm smell—a mixture of soap, heat, and dryer lint. There are labeled laundry bags everywhere. In the corner Harrison finds a big pile of bags stuffed presumably with clean clothes and waggles his eyebrows like a villain in a cartoon.

We're entirely alone.

"Help me," he says.

Huh? I follow him back outside.

Not far from the cabin is an old and crumbling stone

wall. The type of wall farmers built to keep their cows penned. It's hard to imagine that these dark woods used to be field. Harrison hoists several small rocks and hands them to me. When both our arms are full we head back and bury the rocks in the bottom of the bags.

"Jason's supposed to be delivering laundry," Harrison explains. "But he's back at Hostess House partaking in a little illegal activity."

I laugh at the image of the unknown Jason trying to drag these laundry bags and having no idea why they're so heavy.

After a few more trips for rocks, Harrison sits up on a dryer and, well, waits.

It's my move now, but I don't know what to do. Do I sit beside him? Move in between his legs? Just stand here? "So where are you applying this fall?"

He looks at me and then laughs.

"Don't laugh at me," I say, but the question came out of nowhere and, I have to admit, sounded absurd. I laugh too.

So Harrison reaches out his legs and pulls me in. "Where are *you* applying, Miss Nola?"

"I can't remember at the moment," I say, knowing better than to give him my top ten choices.

His fingertips move up and down my arm. "Tell me about your sister," he says.

And I do. I tell him her dreams of being a rock star. How ever since she was a little kid, she's been nocturnal. The rest of us would be sound asleep, and Song would be wandering around the house picking things up and putting them down in new places. The next morning we'd find her curled in a ball somewhere, happy to sleep until noon. It was my job to go around the house each day moving things back.

"Did you mind?"

"Mind?"

"Cleaning up after your sister."

Maybe I did mind. Maybe I never let myself know how much I minded. "At the time I didn't see it that way. I was just doing something I was good at. Like a memory game. I remembered where things belonged."

"You're a good—"

"My dad used to call her Little Bat," I say, and for some reason, this revelation makes me tear up. I miss her more than I realized.

Harrison leans in and kisses my eyelids. Then he barely touches his lips to mine.

I've never been kissed like this, and I want to push myself against him, devour his mouth, but I tell myself to hold, to wait.

And that's when Jason, higher than a kite, comes crashing through the cabin door.

We exchange a delicious look of conspiracy while Jason curses at the weight of the G.D. bags, then Harrison looks at his watch. "You gotta scoot," he says.

Chapter 23

"So how's it going with the charming Harrison?" Kevin asks as I remove dirty dishes from my tray onto his food-globbered counter.

I respond in a Southern accent. "Why, what do you mean, sir?" There are no secrets here at Rocky Cove. It doesn't matter what you try to hold close.

"Going nowhere, huh?"

What can I say? We played a prank together on one of the other counselors? We sorta kissed? Of course, I'd been the one to hunt him down, not the other way around. "Who knows," I say.

"Give it time." He smiles.

It's a nice thing to say. "I'm really sorry I couldn't make the island trip," I tell him.

His face says it all. *Couldn't?*

"Carly made plans—"

His face stays frozen.

I stop the excuses. "You're right, Kevin. It was definitely my loss."

He nods. "Just so we're clear."

"Tell you what. I'll arrange an outing for our next day off. That is—"

"Okay. But there are a few things I require."

"Just give me your list," I say.

Out on the porch Carly is reading aloud from a letter she's received. Mariah is sitting in the next rocker, looking on. Apparently, the pen pal is both funny and artistic—she's drawn pictures in the margins. It takes me a moment to realize that the writer is Song.

"You heard from my sister?" I ask, not bothering to disguise my hurt.

"You didn't?" asks Carly, looking up. She pushes over in her seat. "Here, I'll start again from the beginning."

Song tells Carly how hard it is to be punk when you look like a bald, starving child. No hair to dye black, not enough white blood cells to risk piercing. It's funny, I've never really thought of Song as punk. She's my little sister. I consider her attraction to all things skullish a passing phase. (I can hear Kevin saying, *Punk is so over, Song.*) But I can tell from her letter that she feels taken seriously by

Carly. How many letters has Carly written?

It's a long letter, causing my emotions to waver from curiosity (so this is how Song sounds when she's talking to others), to jealousy (why didn't she tell *me* that?), to guilt (have I been a real friend to Song, or do I just patronize her with my sympathy?). I think of myself as the one with the external experiences and Song as the one with the internal ones, but she's telling Carly her reactions to people in our community, celebrities, my family. She hasn't been living in a bubble after all.

And then I hear this, "'Please keep sending me haiku, Carly. As you know, I collect them. I love that, with haiku, the meaning is between the lines. And you say more between the lines than anyone I know.'"

Up until now there was no collection. For the longest time it's been our own code. Other kids talked in pig Latin, we talked in 5-7-5.

I make some excuse to leave and walk away, feeling numb. Annie is the only one in the barn. She's typing an e-mail, but I can't stop myself from interrupting her. I have to talk to someone.

"I think I'm going out of my mind," I say.

Her fingers stop tapping and she turns to look at me.

"I feel like my life is being taken over . . . by Carly."

"I know what you mean," Annie says. "The barn shrinks over the summer. You should see how Mariah's taken over our room."

"I don't mean stuff," I say, pulling a bench closer. "I mean everything. She has my haircut, she wears my clothes. . . ." *(She steals my ideas, she steals my sister.)*

"But, Nola, Carly is such a good friend to you. And she admires you—anyone can tell. As my mother would say, 'Imitation is the best form of flattery.'"

I take a deep breath. How do I explain? I swallow.

"Talk to her. Tell her how you feel—but do it gently."

"I probably should," I say, even though I know such a conversation would be totally useless.

"You guys have been so close. What would we all do without the Cannolis? There's still plenty of summer left. Don't ruin your friendship for petty reasons."

I nod, suddenly hearing so much more than "Don't ruin *your* friendship." Annie's also saying, *Don't ruin* our *perfect pairing.* We waitresses float two-by-two. When it's time to pick a partner, none of us has to think. When someone needs consoling, we know whose job it is. If Carly and I fall apart, they'd feel pressured to take sides. I feel trapped.

The others have started to stroll in. I thank Annie in a voice that assures her no tantrums will be had and head up to my room. But I'm seething inside. *I'll write Song,* I think. I'll tell *her* my feelings about Carly. Surely, she'll get it.

And then I realize, without a doubt, even that avenue is closed now.

Chapter 24

Next morning, Carly slips her arm through mine as we walk to the docks. "Mariah promised to drive us into Ellsworth after lunch," she says.

"Laundry?" I ask, freeing myself. Unlike the counselors at Robin Hood, Rocky Cove staff has to drive to Scrubbing Bubbles in Ellsworth.

"That, and I would like to buy some shoes. Running shoes. I'm beginning to feel like a slug, sleeping in while you work out. Look at me," she says, pinching her waist. "Every bite I eat is going right to my belly."

"You're not getting fat," I say, trying to keep the edge out of my voice. "You get plenty of exercise. Think of all the hiking we do around here. And you do more swimming than all of us combined."

"I thought you'd be pleased," Carly says, stopping short. "I thought you'd like a running buddy."

Oh, I can't think. My head is muddled. Is it me—or

is it her? "What type of shoes?" I ask finally.

"I don't know. Do you like your New Balances?"

My first reaction is *Ack!* But even *I* know that's ridiculous. Half my cross-country team has the same trainers. It's not the copying that's bothering me this time; it's the awareness that if Carly runs with me, I'll lose the only time I have when my thoughts and feelings are mine alone.

Stop, Nola, I tell myself. *Maybe you're worrying over nothing.* I spread my towel out on the dock. Purchasing shoes does not mean Carly will actually start running.

Mariah invites Annie to Ellsworth too, and after a quick stop at Country View Takeout for their famous blueberry cheesecake ice cream, we look for a place that sells decent trainers.

"You know, this isn't going to be cheap," I say as we pile out of the Volvo outside Willey's Sport Center. "Good running shoes start at about eighty bucks."

"What about poor running shoes?" Carly says. "For the appalling runner?"

Up ahead I see a girl walking into a card shop. I'm not sure—it might be Bridget. It would be easy to go on without checking. And there's a good chance Bridget doesn't want to see me. But I hate the fact that things ended so badly. "Meet you guys in a minute," I say.

"Where are you going?" asks Carly. "I can't pick these out without you."

"I won't be long. See what you like. I'll be right there."

"We can—"

I don't wait for Annie to finish. I pretend to be out of earshot.

It is Bridget. She's looking at baby albums.

"Hi . . . ," I begin.

She jumps, mumbles hi back, and then turns away from me again.

The smell of vanilla and something else (new plastic?) suddenly overwhelms me.

"I just wanted to see how you're doing," I say lamely, reaching for an album—giving my hands something to do. "If everything's okay."

"Everything's peachy," she snaps.

Do I walk away or push forward? "Bridget, I know I wasn't the best roommate, but I don't think I was the worst, either. Why are you so mad?"

She turns toward me, clearly contemplating what to say.

I notice she's beginning to show.

"In a very weak moment I told *one* person I was pregnant," she says. "One person! One person I trusted. That was you."

"And I was okay with it, wasn't I?"

"Yeah. So okay that you felt you could share it with Pete."

It takes me a moment to realize she's accusing me. "I— I didn't—"

"That's why I was fired, Nola."

She doesn't break eye contact, letting this information sink in. "Pete said it was impossible to keep me in light of the fact that I'm in 'a family way.'"

"But I didn't tell him!" I say, ignoring the sounds of other customers around us. Right now it's just me and Bridget.

"How else could he find out?" She's practically yelling too.

I feel sucker punched. "You didn't tell anyone else? Any of the other waitresses?" I ask.

"Did you?" she accuses.

I shake my head, "No. I—"

And then it hits me. I realize I did. My God. My hand, still holding the stupid album, begins to shake. Could Carly have told Pete? If she did, she would have done it by phone. And if so, *she* was responsible for Bridget getting fired. My head is hot. I feel like I'm going to throw up.

"I'm so sorry, Bridget. *I* didn't tell Pete, but I might know who did," I whisper. "I am so, so sorry."

She puts her hands on her belly and gives a little rub. "Carly Whitehouse?" she asks.

"How do you know Carly?" This conversation is getting weird.

"She goes to my high school," Bridget says with a touch of resignation. "Someone told me she was working at Rocky Cove."

"She doesn't go to Winsor? In Boston? Where her mother lives?"

Bridget laughs. "Nope. Deer Isle High. Her mother's the secretary there; father's the basketball coach. Someone said she took off to live with her sister in Boston—she goes to school at—"

"Wendy?"

"Yeah. But I think Wendy wouldn't have any part of it. Sent her home."

"What's her sister like?"

"Really smart . . . and beautiful. Everyone calls her 'the normal one.'"

"You're kidding."

"Carly's crazy, Nola," says Bridget.

"A chameleon?" I ask.

"A pathological liar."

Part of me is shocked. Part of me even wants to defend

her. But most of me is singing, *I know, I know, I know.*

"She was supposedly so wild as a toddler, her parents gave her away for a time. To a grandmother or something. But I don't know if that's true."

I tell Bridget one more time how sorry I am and that I hope she'll let me know when the baby comes.

"Nola," she says as I'm walking out the door.

I turn and look back.

"Be careful."

I decide, as I walk from the card shop to Willey's, not to confront Carly right away. After all, she could have told lots of people on Deer Isle about Bridget and maybe word just got around. So I try to act normal and hope, for once, that Carly can't detect any withdrawal on my part.

"Where did you go?" she whines.

"I thought I might buy a card for Song," I say as cheerfully as I can. "But none seemed right. Which shoes look like you?"

And who are you?

Chapter 25

Truth is, I'm way too afraid to confront Carly. *How crazy is crazy?*

But I have to tell someone. So I beg Kevin (I don't want to tell any of the others just yet) to meet me down at the docks after he's finished washing pots that night.

I ask him: "Do you think she'd actually call to have Bridget fired?" We're sitting at the edge of the dock swatting mosquitoes.

"Well, yeah. Don't you think?" he says.

I laugh. It is such a relief to hear that someone else sees Carly the way I'm beginning—duh!—to see Carly.

"What should I do?"

He slaps a bug on his leg. "Confront her, of course."

"Oh, God, Kevin. I'm too chicken. She could make the rest of my season hell!"

"And how would she do that?"

"I don't know. I feel like if I challenge her on this, she could—I don't know—take away my friends. My job. She did it to Bridget!"

"*Bridget* got pregnant."

"I suppose . . ."

"Harrison?"

"Well, yeah. She's already taken so much that's mine," I say. "Not that Harrison is mine," I quickly add. "It feels like Carly could . . ."

"Could what?" he asks.

"Annihilate me."

Kevin thinks about this. And then he says, "It's true that she is demanding . . . and controlling, but you—"

I stare at him, furious. "You better not be saying this is my fault."

"No. Not in a direct way. I mean—how can I say this? It seems to me that stealing someone's identity and . . . and refusing to claim your own . . ." He pauses.

What? I am suddenly more angry with him than I am with Carly!

He starts again. "Stealing someone's identity and not owning your own—not being *you*—they're the same crime, I think."

"I am being me."

"I don't know. You're being a pale shade of you. Be fierce, Nola."

It's the very thing I say to Song.

He stands. "Now I'm going to go do what *I* was born to do."

I smile, knowing that he means to do a little late-night cooking. "Do you worry about getting caught?" I ask.

"Would I care?"

chapter 26

I seem to have been born with only two speeds: off and on. I can bury my negative reactions beneath layers of justification and self-incrimination, or I can blow with volcanic force, spewing in all directions. (Did I know this before running into Bridget?) Now I'm pushed to on.

We've practiced all day for the play, but Carly, who is supposed to be the understudy, never shows.

"Where've *you* been?" I ask when I head up to our room, after yet another hour-long rehearsal session following the dinner shift.

She's stretched out on her bed, writing something.

"We're performing in two days—you could help, you know."

"Trust me. I can help you with your lines when the time comes," she says. She sits up and acts out my part in one of the scenes, not missing a single word. I know she's performing a scripted part—a part thousands have played—but I feel like she's playing *me*.

"Did you tell Pete that Bridget's pregnant?" I shout.

She stops her performance mid-sentence.

"Did you call Pete?" I ask again.

A slow smile creeps onto her face. She moves so she's crouching on her bed and looks up at me, like a cat ready to be scratched under the chin.

"What did you say to him?"

"I said I was Bridget's closest friend. I told him I was going to be the godmother to her new baby!"

"You impersonated someone else?"

"Brilliant, yes?"

How should I answer that? I should say, *No, Carly. It wasn't brilliant. It was deceitful and manipulative and mean.* But I don't get the chance.

"Don't give me that high-and-mighty look, Nola," she says. "You were thrilled when I showed up here. Remember? Imagine if you had to spend the summer with Bridget." She pauses. "And besides, you and I are exactly the same."

"The *same*?"

"You and me. You *are* me. You go after what you want too, Nola. You're one of the most competitive people I know."

"When have I ever competed with you?" I ask.

She finds this question laughable. "I'll give you credit, Nola. You follow the rules: It's okay to compete, isn't it, as long as you pretend you're not."

"What do you *mean* by 'compete'?"

"'When I use a word, it means just what I choose it to mean, neither more nor less.'"

What?

"*Alice in Wonderland*," she says. "Remember? Humpty Dumpty?"

I'm climbing the face of a cliff; there isn't a foothold, no logic to hold on to. I can't go up. Can't go down.

Mariah flies into the room to tell us there's a party down the road at a summer home.

"Cool," says Carly, as if we were just sitting here thinking of things to do tonight.

"It's ten o'clock," I point out.

"And you're Cinderella," Carly says.

Mariah laughs. She assumes Carly is being playful.

I don't want to go. At this moment I detest Carly. Just being in the same room with her makes me want to scream.

She stands, walks over to the closet, and pulls out the lacy dress she wore when we dug for mussels. "Harrison told me I looked like moonlight last time I had this on. Let's see if he finds me shiny again tonight."

I dig through my pile of clothes to find my favorite tank top. Game's on.

The summer home is within walking distance, but I've never seen it. It's tucked in the trees above a tiny cove, at the end of a long driveway, and I doubt it can be easily seen from the water either. The house itself is spectacular—all polished wood and glass.

At this hour it's packed with kids. The kitchen smells pungent and sweet, a mixture of fruit and spilled beer. A guy I've never seen before says, "You haven't had one yet," and hands me a green icy concoction in a plastic cup. It tastes like key lime pie. "Daiquiri," he says.

"What's in it?" I ask.

"Rum," he answers.

The rest of the rooms smell of sea and pulsating bodies. I walk into one at the front of the house, and there is Carly with Mariah talking to Dom and Harrison. Harrison catches my eye but reveals nothing as he turns back to the others.

Carly seems to be on fire, practically glowing. She pulls Annie into the center of the room, and they start to bend to the music, coaxing the guys to dance with them. Dom matches Carly's movements without hesitation. But Carly's staring at Harrison, pulling him to her with her eyes.

He looks mesmerized.

Do something, I tell myself. *But what?*

I move behind a group of kids, trying to both hide and watch. I clasp my drink with both hands and hold it against my breastbone. I can hardly breathe. I don't want to see what I'm seeing, but I can't turn away.

Carly holds her arms out to Harrison.

He shakes his head and peers around, as if someone just shouted out his name.

I look to see who could be calling him, and when I turn back, he is standing in front of me.

He sets my drink on a shelf and pulls me into the dance crowd. Placing his hands on my hips, he gently moves me from side to side. "Follow me," he says.

I let go. Harrison turns me around—his arm, his hands cross over my body. I lean back—and he's there.

Oh my God. We are synchronized, moving as one person. I face him. He steps back, runs his hands up the back of my neck, through my hair, and cradles my head in his palms, staring at me as we move. His eyes don't leave mine. It's more than I can take. I don't think. I kiss him.

He kisses back. His mouth's salty and sweet, tender and demanding. I want to stay locked like this forever. No, in truth, I want to be swallowed up by him.

But instead, I do something very, very stupid.

I look over to see how Carly's reacting.

Harrison follows my eyes. He sees the intensity between me and Carly—sees that we're entangled in some sort of contest. It takes only a moment for me to look from Carly back to Harrison, but that moment is too telling. He drops his arms and backs away . . . then wiggles toward Mariah.

I don't know what to do. He's dancing. He won't glance back. So I turn and leave, running up the dirt driveway, eyes so full of tears, I bang into someone walking down.

"Whoa," Kevin says.

"Sorry," I say, and try to run by him, but he grabs the back of my shirt. He pulls me into a hug, and I sob into his tank shirt until it's soaked.

"Has someone hurt you?" he asks.

I shake my head. "Not exactly."

"Boy trouble?"

I nod.

"No matter," he says.

Why? Please, Kevin. Have the magic words to help me go back and straighten this all out.

"I was coming to get you," he says. "You've got company."

chapter 27

There, standing in the center of the barn's rec room, is my sister. I look around, expecting to see my parents, but it hits me that Song has come alone.

"Surprise!" she shouts.

"Do Mom and Dad know you're here?"

"Thanks a lot, Nola. I'm happy to see you too."

Both of us look at Kevin as if he should somehow be the judge of what's appropriate at this moment.

He gives a double-handed wave and backs out the door.

"I *am* happy to see you, Song—"

"No, you're not. I can see it written all over your face. I should have known you wouldn't be."

"Why? You know—"

"Carly—"

My phone rings. It's Dad. Parents are frantic. They just discovered that Song is not with my aunt, as she told them she would be.

"She's here, Dad. Just barely arrived. No, of course not. No, I did not know. Let me call you in a few."

"Come here." I hug her, feel her relax.

She tells me how Carly thought it would be a great idea to come and see me in the play, how she purchased her own bus ticket and even arranged for a cab to bring her from Bangor to Rocky Cove.

"That must have cost a fortune!" I say.

"The guy didn't charge me."

I pull free, give Song my evil eye. It didn't take long for her to learn that she could play the tumor card. When she went bald the first time, she started going after anything she wanted. Maybe she thought it was her right—payback for what she was going through.

She grabs my hands. "Please let me stay, Nola. I really, really, really want to see you in the play. And you know how chemo is. I feel like crap at first, but by the time I'm getting close to my next treatment, I'm back to being myself."

"When's your next appointment?"

"In a few days. Have to be back on Monday."

I am totally torn. There is a part of me that still wants Rocky Cove to be *my* place—even as screwed up as things are tonight. I feel like I'm just beginning to figure out who I want to be, but with Song here, I'm apt to go right back to being . . . *who?* The invisible one. But she's only asking for a few days.

Song detects a crack. "Please, Nola. Mom and Dad will listen to you. *You* needed a break. I feel that way too. I'll do anything to get away from my room, boring daytime TV, and pills—just for a few days. Besides, I miss you, Nola."

She's got me. I call Mom and Dad to plead her case. I promise them that I will take extraordinary care. I'll take time off so I can be with Song every minute.

It's not easy. After discussing every obstacle, every precaution under the sun, my mother has a brainstorm: "We'll come too," she says. "We'll come and see you in the play."

I think about this for a moment, staring at Song. She hasn't looked at me this way since I was ten years old and holding our dead goldfish. She was, of course, willing me to make it live again. I let her down then. I don't want to let her down now.

"I think that might be defeating the purpose," I say. Maybe, I tell my mother, maybe if Song has just a few days to feel independent, the rest of the summer might not be quite so bad.

Mom confers with my father. Song can stay for two nights—counting tonight. Just two.

She won't get to see the play, but she'll catch the dress

rehearsal. I share the news, prepared to be her hero.

She jumps up and down and asks, "So where's Carly?"

We move her bag to my room. I tell her twice we're not going to the party. "Carly isn't the friend you think she is," I say, my voice barely above a whisper.

"You're wrong," she says, resting her head on Carly's pillow. "What do you know? You haven't read our letters! You didn't invite me to come here to Maine. *She* did!"

I hear voices and look out the front window. There's a crowd, but Carly is lagging behind with Harrison. She looks up, sees me. Then she reaches out, grabs Harrison, and kisses him.

I have no idea if he kisses back. I do know he doesn't push her away. He looks up and sees me too.

That is that.

"Carly's back," I say to Song.

She can hardly contain herself. "Surprise!" she yells, springing up from the cot as Carly comes into the room.

Carly looks confused for a moment and then embraces Song like her oldest and dearest friend. "God, you look so gorgeous!" she says, rubbing her hand along Song's head. "I'm going to shave my head too."

I don't doubt it.

Chapter 28

We're at breakfast. Mom has already called twice. I assure her that I gave up my bed, that Song had a good night's sleep.

"So where did your name come from?" Nigel asks my sister.

Carly leans in close and eats a blueberry off Song's plate.

"Hey," says Song. "My real name is Sonya," she says, "but Nola was four when I was born and thought my name was Song."

Everyone agrees that "Song" is a cool mistake.

"But I will call you 'Poet' because that is what you are," says Carly. "You should hear some of her haiku," she says to the others. "Right, Nola?"

"Right," I say, the Nola puppet. She's just making sure I remember.

———

Pete calls me into the office as soon as I have finished up with my tables that morning. He reminds me that there's a policy—waitresses are not allowed to have overnight guests, nor are guests allowed to accompany waitresses to staff meals.

I apologize and tell him about my sister's unexpected arrival. We agree that I'll arrange for others to cover my tables, give up my next two days off, and have a percentage of my pay cut to cover the cost of Song's meals.

Welcome to the real world, Nola.

"Like I eat anything!" says Song, flopped down on my bed.

"I think Pete's being pretty generous, Song," I tell her. "He's already breaking two of the rules for you."

"He's charging her!" says Carly, wiggling out of her uniform. "Song is now a paying guest and should be treated like one. You can eat in the dining room, Song!" says Carly. "I'll be your waitress!"

Song looks at Carly as if she is creating the only patch of sun in a very chilly forest.

I leave the room to shower. When I return, Carly and Song are gone.

"Don't change into your suit, Nola," says Lucy. "We want to get in another run-through before the dress rehearsal this afternoon."

"The dress is not tonight?"

"Nope," Brita says, popping out of her room to join the conversation. Her eyes tell me something big is up.

Ledges.

I can't concentrate. Where did Carly take Song? I promised my parents I'd look after my sister, but now I have no idea where she is.

"Of course you do," Lucy says, not unkindly. "They're at the docks—right where we'd be if we weren't here."

"What else is there to do at ten thirty in the morning?" says Brita.

They're right. No doubt Carly and Song are in the sun—oh, shit. The sun.

I tell the others that I'll be right back. I run upstairs, grab my tube of sunscreen, and take off for the docks.

"Are you running at this hour?" Carly asks when I arrive.

"No. I just thought Song might have forgotten this." I hold out the tube of sunscreen but feel like a total jerk. Song is covered head to foot in fabrics—loose, flowing pants and a light silky top of Carly's. She even has a hat on. She looks as funky and artistically cool as Carly did the first day I met her.

Song rolls her eyes at Carly.

Carly smiles. "She tries," she says.

I've performed only my opening lines during dress rehearsal when Carly and Song skip out again. *Damn it!*

But what can I do? I can't stop the rehearsal and chase after them—we have guests, including Mrs. Barnes, who are watching this afternoon's run-through instead of squeezing in tomorrow night.

I think of Song saying she came all that way to watch me in the play, and it burns.

No doubt Carly is *trying* to anger me. I won't let her have the satisfaction. I put in my best performance so far.

It's weird, but when you're acting—being someone else—you not only escape your own life, you actually get to experience the present more fully. It must have something to do with acceptance, I think. We accept who we're pretending to be (it's just pretend, right?) so we don't judge. We just are.

"Yoo-hoo, Miss Nola," whispers Kevin, calling me back to my part.

Whoops, looks like neither Vera nor Nola was present in that moment.

We're just about to wrap things up for dinner when Harrison walks into the barn.

"Can we help you?" Nigel asks.

Harrison catches my eye, but I don't move. I admit it, up until last night I harbored the hope that he would choose me. But I know better now. I'm embarrassed by my foolishness and look down. When I look up again, he's gone.

Obviously. The one he was looking for wasn't here.

Kevin comes to me, puts his hand on the back of my neck, and squeezes.

The rest of the cast circles around me. They know just what to do. Instead of mumbling things like, *He's not worth it, Nola,* they talk about how funny and lively the play is going to be. They tell me that the guests are never going to see me as just one of the Cannolis again.

And I realize for the first time that summer that I don't belong just because Carly made it possible. In another twenty-four hours my sister will be gone, Harrison and Carly will likely be hanging out in the grotto, but I will still be a part of this place, one of these friends.

Chapter 29

Before I begin the dinner shift, Pete sends Nigel up to get me—to have me come to the office. This time I'm panicked. Is Song all right? I haven't seen her all afternoon. Once when we were younger, and staying on Gotts Island, Song wandered away from where we were sitting on the beach. I'll never forget the fear on my parents' faces (a look that would reappear many more times in later years). I feel that same agonizing worry as I race down the hill, leaving Nigel behind.

I can hear my mother's voice from our phone call last night: *This isn't a simple babysitting job, Nola—this is life and death. You know that.*

But Pete doesn't want to talk about my sister at all. He wants to tell me that Mr. Winston said they'd miss me these two days—that I've been providing them with exceptional service. "Really," said Pete. "You've been their favorite waitress." He says it as though he's surprised.

I laugh. "I guess they've had some bad experiences in the past," I say.

Pete laughs too. "You did have a rough start," he says. "But you work hard, Nola. I appreciate that. Thought you should know that others do too."

Carly and Song appear at the staff dinner talking of blueberry picking and a trip to the infamous dump where seagulls flock in huge numbers—clouds of flapping white scavengers. I have yet to do either of these things and feel a bite of jealousy. But at the same time I can't deny that Carly has made the day special for Song. I look at Carly and see the girl I swam with on her first night here, the girl who created our mermaid's den, and feel an unexpected pang of sadness.

Song and I head up to the barn while the others wait dinner, and she lies down on my bed. I can see she's tired. Her skin is even paler than usual and she has dark circles under her eyes.

"Don't you even think of jumping off the ledges tonight," I tell her. I am part serious, part joking. She is the least likely to jump. She doesn't like heights any more than I do, and unlike me, she's never had the opportunity to become a good swimmer.

"I thought Harrison was your boyfriend," she says, ignoring my order.

"I didn't say that."

"Carly told me that he's always had a thing for her. That she tried not to encourage him, but it didn't change his feelings. He kissed her, you know."

"I know, Song. Last night. While I was up here with you."

I watch this fact register. "So is it *my* fault?" she asks, suddenly alarmed.

"God, no!" Tears spring from my eyes. "That's not what I meant at all. Of course it's not your fault. Move over," I say, and lie down next to her. We stare at the ceiling the way we do at home when it gets too hard to figure anything out.

"You smell like fried fish," she says.

"I know."

When I come out of the shower, Carly has appeared. "Better hurry up," she says. "Or you'll miss the first jump."

"We're not going," I say, pulling out my sweats, feeling a moment of solidarity between me and my sister.

"You wouldn't make Song miss this, would you? This is her last night, Nola. Song-o-lo, you didn't come all this way to stay in your big sister's room."

Song sits up. "I could just go and watch, Nola." She

reaches into her backpack and pulls out one of her multitudinous skull shirts.

I have a queasy feeling. I hear Bridget's warning: *Nola, be careful.* And I want to pull Song close, protect her—not from the ledges, but from the likes of Carly Whitehouse.

Song is looking at me with open, pleading eyes. How can I refuse?

"Let me get dressed," I say.

"We're ready," says Carly. "Right, Song? We'll meet you there."

Chapter 30

I have to find my sister.

It isn't hard. I had expected her to be standing somewhere at the wood's edge watching kids cajole one another into jumping. Instead, Song seems to be at the center of a group of counselors with the sea as her backdrop.

I look at Mariah for some sort of explanation.

"They're from another boys' camp," she explains. "Visiting Robin Hood. Dom brought them over."

Carly is standing next to Song, her hands stretched toward her as if to say, *Behold my lovely specimen.*

I move in, expecting Song to be sharing some opinion on the best alternative band or maybe doing one of her spoofs about doctors and hospitals.

But no, Carly is egging her on to recite haiku. "Do the one about the skydiver," she says.

Song takes a deep breath:

"He finally jumps

Plunging, diving toward earth

Whoops! Can't find the string"

Oh, God. The crowd is silent.

Except for Carly. "Come on, guys! You know that was funny!"

The last line is funny—but in a little-kid, pathetic way. Most don't know what to do. They don't want to encourage her (it's too embarrassing), and they definitely don't want to hurt a bald kid's feelings.

"Do the one about the love note!" Carly says, all the time smiling at the guys.

Just then Harrison arrives with his goggles and towel. "What's going on?"

No one says anything.

Song looks to Carly for direction.

"Keep going," says Carly.

Song recites:

"Recognizable

Your printing will always be

'Cause I heart you too"

Even I cringe without meaning to.

Dom counts the syllables out on his fingers. "Yup! It's haiku," he says.

"Wow!" says Jason, the guy from the laundry shack. It's sarcasm, intended to go over Song's head.

Carly laughs. "Give her a topic," she says. "She can do these on the spot."

"Let's dive," says Harrison.

My throat catches. *Doesn't he know this is Song? Doesn't he care?*

"Poseur," Carly says slowly, looking directly at me. "That's your topic. Poseur."

"What do you mean?" asks Song.

"You know," she says, turning back to her. "Someone who's pretending to be something she's not. Like someone pretending to be punk."

"Ouch," says someone in the crowd.

"She's only a kid," shouts Lucy.

"Poseur," says Carly. "That's your haiku topic."

Song suddenly seems undressed, raw—out of her league. Her face registers confusion. The word "poseur, poseur, poseur," moves over her lips. She steps back, but there's nowhere to go.

I can't stand it. Pretending to be a photographer:

> *"Stop, poser, hold that*
> *So beautiful, beautiful*
> *The camera loves you"*

I lean into Song with exaggerated movements, begging her to follow me.

> *"Turn again this way*
> *Talk to the camera, baby*
> *Favorite poser"*

"How do you do that?" Annie says.

I do have speed.

Song stares at me. I don't know if she's going to run, lash out, or trust. I do know that she can do this. *Come on, my eyes say to her. This is us, Song. You and me. We can take this moment up.*

"Speaking of poseur . . . ," says Carly, looking at me. "Who's going to dive?"

The night is still.

Song looks at Carly. Then she takes a breath and wags her finger at me:

> *"Call me a poser*
> *But inauthentic, fakey?*
> *Definitely not"*

I smile and hold up my pretend camera.

Moving like a model, she performs again:

> *"Do not define me*
> *By anything other than*
> *What I choose to be"*

I see Harrison counting on his fingers.

It scans, I want to shout at him. My sister is smart.

He looks up and sees me glaring at him.

Holding eye contact, he comes forward. He turns, stands next to us, and slowly recites:

> *"Suppose, you could pose*
>
> *As anyone you wanted"*

He stops, counts on his fingers, and then:

> *"I would choose brave too"*

Oh my God. Did he just do that? The crowd gives a whoop.

Now lots of kids are counting syllables, trying to compose their own, competing for airtime.

I look at Harrison with intense gratitude.

He looks back at me with something brand new. Something so strong and so sweet, my first impulse is to hide.

But I hear my sister's name again and turn.

Carly is peeling off her clothes.

I cry and reach out, reach for an arm, for fingers—

Too late.

Carly grabs Song's hand and, running, yanks her off the edge of the cliff and into the breaking waves below.

Chapter 31

Never mind that I'm a chicken who's never had the courage to high dive. I leap in after her. I slice feetfirst into the frigid ocean and surface as quickly as I can. Bodies land like bombs all around me, making it impossible to see. My clothes are wet and heavy, weighing me down. I can barely catch my breath. I unzip my pants and kick out of them while calling, "Song . . . Song . . . Song."

"Nola!" It's Harrison. He's got my sister in a lifeguard hold, and he's taking her in——not to the rocky shore, where it would be hard to climb, but to the nearest beach.

I swim after them.

I'm crying as I wrap my arms around my little sister, thanking Harrison over and over.

Song is frightened and shaking, but she lets me hold her.

Carly's voice can be heard over the others, instigating a game of Marco Polo. She's not thinking one thought about Song at this moment.

I grab a towel left behind by a guest and wrap it around Song. Then the three of us begin climbing the hill.

"They were making fun of me."

"They're jerks," Harrison says.

She stops. "Not all of them," says Song.

That's it. I can't hear one more word. I thank Harrison again for his help and practically drive Song up to the barn. "We've got to get you dry," I say.

"They're not all jerks, Nola," she says again.

Still I ignore her.

"But Carly is."

Chapter 32

Song is dry and warm—but too warm. She looks gray, and I'm pretty certain she has a fever. I know I have failed her, failed my parents. Do I find Pete to bring her into the Blue Hill hospital? Do I try to get her home? I decide that the worst thing would be to keep my parents in the dark. I call home.

"I'm so sorry, Mom." I'm crying before I can even tell her the details. But she and my father are practiced. They go into emergency mode. Any anger will be saved for later. They ask if we can find a ride south. They will meet us partway.

I run back to the ledges to find someone with a car. I'm approaching Annie—to see if she knows where Mariah is—when Carly jumps out of the crowd and asks, "How's that sweet little Song?"

"She's sick, Carly. Seriously sick."

Carly nods her head and then lowers her voice and speaks slowly, as if to calm an irrational drama queen. "A bad night?"

"You just plunged her into the Atlantic Ocean, Carly. She's fighting cancer and she can't swim. What the hell do you think?"

Annie giggles. A nervous giggle.

"I think she's fine, Nola. She'll talk about the experience for the rest of her life. Maybe," Carly says, turning to walk away from me, "maybe you need to start thinking about what she *really* needs instead of trying to make yourself feel important."

"Carly!" I shout.

She turns back around. "What?" She stands there impatiently.

I don't know what. *I'll unveil all her secrets—expose her for who she is. I'll . . .*

And then I can't help it. I burst out laughing. A belly-splitting laugh. In the past half hour I have gone from panic, to tears, to anger, to craziness. "Nothing," I snort. "Just nothing."

Carly walks off.

Annie looks at me as if I'm insane, but I know I'm more sane at this moment than I've been all summer. Suddenly, I see Carly as . . . sad. Not as strong, but weak. Someone to pity. Someone with no power over me at all.

———

I find Mariah, but she's already tipsy.

So I race through the crowd to find Kevin. "How much have you had to drink?" I ask. If he's been drinking, I'll have to ask Pete.

"Hardly anything," he says. "I just got here. Missed a good performance, I heard."

He doesn't hesitate to say yes—the distance doesn't matter. We'll drive until we meet up with my parents.

The three of us sit in the front of Kevin's truck, Song huddled between us. She dozes on and off. I keep in constant contact with my parents by cell phone.

They meet us at a Panera right off the highway in Augusta. Mom takes the sleeping bag I've kept wrapped around Song and hands it back to me. "I'll call you," she says.

"What do you mean?" I say. "I'm not going back." I hadn't even thought of what comes next—my only goal was to reach my parents. But at this moment I know what I'm saying is true.

"No, Nola," cries Song. "You have to go back. You have to be in the play. You have to talk to Harrison again!"

"You have your job, Nola," says my father.

I stop to think. Is it right to break my commitments? What about my job, the play? What about the rest of the summer? I think of all that might happen if I do return.

And then I look at my sister and know I will have no regrets.

"Pete will understand," I say. "And Carly knows every single one of my lines—she'll happily take over for me. I'm staying with Song."

"Don't let me wreck this for you," Song says.

"You're not. I'm not staying because I think I should. I'm staying because this is what I choose—this is where *I* want to be." We don't have the time or energy to argue. I walk Kevin back to his truck.

"You're a very good friend," I tell him.

"I know," he says. "And you know what, Nola?"

"What?"

"You so deserve me."

I hug him long and hard.

Somehow we come to believe that life gives us what we deserve. But that isn't true, is it? Does Song deserve to be sick?

Song sleeps until we reach the Boston area, and then she whispers, "Tell me a story—a Rocky Cove story."

I decide to tell her about the night before she arrived at Rocky Cove. How everyone had spontaneously congregated, after a rehearsal, in the dining room late at night.

We sat at the messy tables and retold silly summer stories. Kevin had made cream puffs with ice cream and fudge sauce. If Pete and Susanna heard us hanging out in the inn, they didn't shoo us out. And then, wouldn't you know it, Cheffie walked in. Walked over to the tables and looked down at the food there. Food from *his* kitchen. He didn't say a word. He just reached out and grabbed a cream puff from the platter. "Damn good," he said, and walked out. We all cheered.

"Was Carly there?"

"Yes, she was there." But I don't tell Song that Carly accused me of acting tired and bored—precisely the opposite of what I was feeling. Someday I will tell Song the complete history of why I hate Carly Whitehouse, but not tonight.

Chapter 33

The hospital is quiet at this hour and could feel quite frightening. But it is so familiar to all of us, being back almost feels like coming home. Song is immediately hooked up to tubes and monitors. It turns out she has an infection—an infection that was likely growing in her when she came to Rocky Cove but was exacerbated by lack of sleep and the cold ocean. Her body lost the energy to fight it. She has to stay here at General for an indefinite amount of time, and her chemo sequence will have to be changed again.

I blame myself, my parents blame themselves, but Song tells us to cut it out, it's not fair. Other teenagers get blamed for doing stupid, irresponsible things—she'd be a lot happier if we'd do what we're supposed to do and blame her. "Geesh," she says. "Give me a little credit for acting out, won't you?"

But she looks so little and fragile. I read to the end of *Pride and Prejudice*, which was tucked in my purse, and watch her sleep.

Near dawn, before the breakfast rush, I call the inn to tell Pete I won't be back. As predicted, he's pretty understanding, and he calls back a few hours later to say not to worry, my stuff will be delivered to my front door. Thank God I packed light.

Over the next few days, when I'm not at the hospital, I'm on the computer reading messages from Rocky Cove. The performance was a huge success, though everyone has been really careful to play it down. They know how much I was looking forward to the big night.

Nigel attaches photos he took this summer, and in a short note says he made the decision to defer his acceptance to Colgate. He probably won't return to Rocky Cove next summer either. He wants to try something new, to set his own course. Go, Nigel!

Susanna mails pictures from Stella—one for me and one for Song.

I feel stabbed when I recall what I'm missing. I think of Carly getting to play Vera and I feel downright murderous. Then I think of Harrison and the way he looked at me after reciting the haiku, and I come close to crying.

Carly hasn't communicated with me at all. But I guess after our last conversation that's to be expected.

Annie has hinted at the fact that she's losing her best Rocky Cove friend to Carly. I want to warn Annie, to warn Mariah, but would it make a difference? I doubt it.

But when I'm hit with pangs of longing—longing for Rocky Cove—I remind myself that what I want most in the world is for Song to get better and that I'm here not because this is the life I've been handed or the life I've been forced to live, but because this is the life that *is* mine.

"Can I pull you away from that computer?" my mother asks, standing in my bedroom doorway.

"Nope," I say, kidding.

"Not even to tell you that someone's here with your things?"

"Someone's here?" Kevin, I immediately know. I thought Pete was sending my stuff by UPS. I fly down the stairs.

So when I get to the front door, my heart stops. So does my breathing. I don't know what to say.

Chapter 34

Harrison.

"Bet you didn't expect me," he says, and just stands there on my front stoop, grinning.

"I had no idea. You have my stuff?"

"Yup."

"But——," I say, searching for something, anything to understand how this camp counselor from Maine could end up on my steps in Walpole, Massachusetts. "But that's not very Taoist," I say.

"No." He laughs and then looks me in the eye. "But I haven't been myself since you left."

I sit down on the step. I'd invite him in, but after introductions and small talk with my parents, I might never get to actually talk to him.

He asks about Song, and then he sits down beside me. "I really blew it this summer, Nola. I knew that this was my last summer at Robin Hood. I was so determined it would be perfect, and, well, it became the summer of my missed opportunity."

I force myself to ask the question. "What about Carly?"

"There's something about Carly, isn't there?" he says. "She's so—I don't know—out there."

He hasn't answered my question.

"Okay, I was curious about her. Maybe even attracted." He blushes. I've never seen Harrison blush.

"But I couldn't help feeling she wasn't being straight—there was something manipulative about her," he says. "It was like I smelled a rat and I was going to poke it out."

"And how were you planning on doing that?" I ask.

"I don't know. At first I relied on my charms. But," he says, laughing, "they're obviously not very effective. After a while I think I was annoyed. I saw her as an opponent."

"You were smarter than I was. I thought she was wonderful."

"I know. And since we're being truthful . . . ," he says, looking at me.

I can tell he's trying not to offend, and so I brace myself.

"That's what made me guarded around you. I mean, it was like you guys were trying to be twins or something."

I look away and notice the cracks in our walkway, the

dying plants on the borders for the very first time. I can't deny it. True, Carly played a big part in that—but I was so willing to . . . what's the word?

Follow.

"And she was so weirdly possessive of you. I didn't know if I cared enough to cross that line," Harrison says.

I have no defense. Nevertheless, I start to say *sorry*—and then, remembering, stop myself.

He turns my face to look at him. "But then I watched you that night with your sister, and, I don't know, I saw *you*."

Harrison used his day off to come and tell me that. So even though he could only stay through dinner, and even though I don't know when we'll get the chance to see each other again, he has given me a huge present. (And a promise to write.)

There are some people who are born into this world—like Harrison, maybe—knowing exactly who they are.

And there are the Carlys, who, like hermit crabs, are always looking to find a home in someone else's shell.

And then, I suppose, there are the rest of us. People like me. People who, for whatever reason, don't quite know their shape. Don't know their boundaries. When you're in this position, it's hard to stop others from rushing in to fill up the space with, ironically, themselves.

Like Song—like everyone, really—I live with uncertainty. But, as corny as it sounds, with each new decision *I* make, I'm given a chance.

A chance to learn what it means to be me.

Huh.

Carly gave me that.